All
Things
Irish

A Novel

A tale about life, love, and bad Irish luck
—the best kind there is.

MICHAEL LOYND

Praise for *ALL THINGS IRISH*:

"A charming and thoughtful read that should prove hard to overlook."—*Midwest Book Review*

"A lively, dexterously written novel."—*St. Louis Beacon*

"I loved every page! How could you not? Charming, poignant, funny, and so genuinely Irish."—**Patti McCoy Jacob, book critic**

"Tearfully poignant one moment and laugh out funny the next, *All Things Irish* sparkles with a razor-sharp wit and some of the most colorful, honest and original characters to grace the pages of a novel since P.G. Wodehouse or Fannie Flagg."—**Paul Guyot, television writer,** *Judging Amy,* *Leverage*

"A fresh and joyous recipe of life, love and family. Take a big, wonderful bite and savor every delicious moment!"
—**Bart Baker, author,** *Honeymoon with Harry* **(soon to be a major motion picture from New Line/Warner Bros.)**

"This book is a delightful story that portrays the conflicted, spiritual, superstitious, dark, self-deprecating, cynical, and playful Irish, including second-, third-, fourth- and fifth-generation O'mericans. Blending these characters with mountain goats and cartoonish Scandinavians in Door County is a clever premise that unfolds as solid entertainment."—*Read Village*

DISCLAIMER

This is a work of fiction. Names, characters, places and incidents either are products of the author's imagination or are used fictitiously. Any resemblance to actual events or locales or persons, living or dead, is entirely coincidental.

Published by Writers' Press
13321 N. Outer 40 Rd., Ste. 100
Town and County, MO 63017

To my wife Katie, Raz, Oma, and Nana—four of the greatest women I've known

ACKNOWLEDGMENTS

I want to give special thanks to Maura Lawler, at the Kerry Cottage in St. Louis, her late-mother Mary, and Megan O'Meara, at O'Meara's Irish House in Door County, for sharing all their wonderful stories. To the Fitzsimmons, for all the great memories of Door County, and the Murphys, for their generous long-term loan of their Door County book collection. To Meg Huber and Colleen Krentz, for their stories of working in Irish shops. To Mr. K, the Big Irishman. To my mother's tightknit group of friends (whose lifelong sisterhood continues to inspire). To the Walz side. To all of my incredible aunts (especially Toni). To my sisters and sister-in-laws. To great friends in Baxter Ridge and all the Halloweeners. To Bart Baker, Joe Reinkemeyer, and Paul Guyot, friends and mentors. To David Montgomery. To Jeroen Ten Berge, for his great design talents. To Cynthia Andreyuk, my wonderful editor. To Oma and Raz, for your unmatched enthusiasm. To Irish shop owners everywhere who give year-round life to this wickedly fun Irish subculture. To the great people of Door County, who keep the Northern Peninsula special.

"Life is difficult. This is a great truth, one of the greatest truths. It is a great truth because once we truly see this truth, we transcend it. Once we truly know that life is difficult - once we truly understand and accept it - then life is no longer difficult. Because once it is accepted, the fact that life is difficult no longer matters."

—*The Road Less Travelled*
by M. Scott Peck (honorary Irishman)

CHAPTER 1

THE FISH IN THE IRISH SWEATER

There is one race of people for whom psychoanalysis is of no use whatsoever.

—Sigmund Freud on the Irish

THE ONLY THING THE VILLAGERS of Whitefish Creek feared more than any little change to their quaint Wisconsin fishing hamlet was change instituted by outsiders. So on that cold February day, when a fish wandered into the Door County Realty office and bought their beloved Olsson House, shockwaves rattled the tiny lakeside community.

For over 100 summers, the 1½-story vacant cottage greeted visitors to Whitefish Creek's charming history of Nordic cross flags, troll statues, fish boils, Norwegian hospitality, and rich Scandinavian architecture and décor.

Tourists delighted in seeing the cottage's historic, Norwegian-style, sod-covered roof, stopping their cars, standing in the street, pointing, smiling, and snapping pictures at the three 10-foot-tall fir trees that grew on top. Olsson House featured prominently in every Door County brochure, until the uninvited fish painted its Norwegian-red walls cream, removed the wooden Swedish Dala horse that hung off its roadside post, and next committed the sin of all sins by sticking a big obnoxious Irish flag out front.

No one knew from where the fish came.

The few residents who encountered the unwelcome fish spoke of her Irish accent.

One person claimed she saw her under the full moonlight whistling a jig and dancing barefoot in the snow.

The villagers called her a gypsy, a raider, a vandal, a kook.

Some even accused her of witchcraft.

But one thing for certain, she was definitely a FISH— the acronym Door Countians called anyone not locally born and raised with several generations of Scandinavian relatives buried up on yonder hillside. Generally speaking, the moniker affably referred to outsiders. More directly, tourists. But at its most disparaging, F-I-S-H stood for "F*#!ing Illinois Shit Heads." Or in this case—"Fookin' Irish."

The hated flag threatened the livelihoods of every local merchant who thrived on the town's pristine Scandinavian persona that attracted nearly three million summer tourists a year.

And the panicked villagers wasted no time plotting to run this unwanted FISH out of town.

CHAPTER 2

LUCK O' THE IRISH

If you're lucky enough to be Irish, you're lucky enough.

—*Irish saying*

THIRTY-YEAR-OLD MEG MCKENNA could not believe the train wreck her mother set in motion. Until now, Meg was always the failure of the family, with certain mistakes Meg would never live down in her mother's eyes. But this imminent disaster seemed too ridiculous for even Meg's standards.

Sure, her mother had talked about opening an Irish shop for as long as anyone remembered, carting all six children around the Midwest to *feiseanna* (Irish dance competitions) and scrutinizing other wannabe Irish vendors in a brogue as thick as a pint of Guinness: "Oi loike dat;" "Oi don't loike dat;" "wasn't dat lovely;" or "no self-respectin' Oirishman would sell such gaudy trinkets." She insisted her shop would house only the finest Waterford crystal and Belleek china. Sell only the thickest Aran sweaters and beautiful Claddagh jewelry. None of those tacky *Kiss Me I'm Irish* buttons, or obnoxious leprechaun hats or beer huggies. Those catered strictly to "Plastic Paddies," she insisted, those fourth and subsequent generation O'mericans whose only sense of heritage was taking one day out of the year to cover themselves in green (a ridiculous cliché her mother admonished as the most unlucky color for any true Irishman) and celebrate a total fraud like St. Patrick (who her mother swore was neither Irish, nor named Patrick, nor an officially canonized saint).

Even Meg, in her younger days, humored her mother's infectious pipedream, brainstorming over fresh-baked Irish soda bread about the shop's appearance and what wonderful Celtic things to offer. But that was before Meg's mistakes tore them apart. Before her mother could not forgive. Before Meg wanted nothing more to do with her mother's crazy shamrock-shaped world.

But an Irish shop! In Door County! From a woman without retail experience.

It would not end well.

Meg was being evicted from her Los Angeles apartment when her five older siblings and godmother Mary Lou Fitzgibbons (her mother's 55-year-old best friend and partner in crime) flooded her with pleas to go to Door County and help her mother.

Meg lost everything over the last few years, including a swanky Rodeo Drive retail job when the recession hit. She spent the prior few years struggling to make ends meet with a series of unreliable retail jobs, temp work, and waitressing. She started a vintage clothing store with a "friend" who ran up a joint credit card to the tune of $10,000, skipped town with the last of their cash, and left Meg to face the music.

Now all Meg possessed was an old Volkswagen Bug on life support, a horrible credit score, a mountain of debt, a nonexistent love life, and a washed-up acting career that was more about self-therapy as she desperately continued to search for her true calling. After a decade of hearing she was not thin enough, not busty enough, not sexy enough, not talented enough, and more recently, too old—Meg's acting reached its end at age thirty. Her highlight was a five-month gig on a second-rate soap seven years earlier and a small blurb in "Soap Opera Digest" noting her dazzling smile. Many considered her pretty, but not the drop-dead Hollywood starlet level. She was thin for the Midwest, but not the West Coast. Her long amber hair never seemed to cooperate. And her agency of eight years just dumped her. The only reason her manager Irene hadn't followed suit was because Meg was the least neurotic of all her clients.

"Listen," Irene said. "I'm always in your corner. But life has a way of giving you signs. And you need to listen to them. Trust me, this town will take your best years and spit you out. You got the talent and toughness. But the people who make it in this town also have damn good luck. And you've never had any of that. Go back to the Midwest and find a good life while you still can."

Not the pep talk Meg hoped for, but she could not argue about her rotten luck.

Her mother always swore if there was such a thing as the "luck o' the Irish" it was all bad—and that, she insisted, was a good thing.

Meg could've been the poster child for this cursed Irish birthright. But she had yet to see how bad Irish luck was ever a good thing.

Meg needed to regroup. She wanted a temporary escape from Los Angeles to rethink her life.

A brother in Seattle offered a refuge to clear her head, as did her brother in Charlottesville, her brother in Atlanta, her brother in Houston, and her sister in Boston. Even her godmother Mary Lou offered a free room. The only one who didn't was her crazy Irish mother, who recently buried a statue of St. Joseph in the backyard of their St. Louis home (a Catholic superstition to sell a house fast), sold it off after 30 years of memories, and drove nine hours north to squander every last penny she ever saved to start this Irish boondoggle.

But Meg also knew her mother was in trouble.

They shared a sixth sense with each other. Even though estranged these past few years, Meg felt her pain.

Meg's five older siblings were busy worrying about their own families. Which left Meg the only one capable of dropping everything to help (the penalization for not marrying and pumping out a litter of kids).

The last decade, Meg and her mother mixed about as well as a pint of black-and-tan. Even the simplest conversations escalated into World War III.

But now her mother needed Meg's help, whether she admitted it or not. And even though reentering her mother's insane Irish world was the last thing Meg wanted, it was a family thing. And that weighed on Meg's conscience like an elephant.

Meg packed her belongings into her old Volkswagen Bug that had a piece of plywood covering a hole in the driver's-side floorboard and embarked upon the three-day drive towards Wisconsin, secretly hoping her car would die before she ever reached her mother.

CHAPTER 3

THE DOOR COUNTIAN

Wisconsin's Largest Twice-Weekly Newspaper

Featured Columnist...
Seneca Parks

Historical Society Declares War on Leprechauns

THE SALE OF WHITEFISH CREEK'S Olsson House ignited a firestorm between the Door County Historical Society and the home's new owner, Mrs. Moira "Mo" McKenna. The Historical Society's president, Mrs. Emmeline Elefsson, claims that Mrs. McKenna's Irish shop constitutes the worst historical desecration since the demolition of the old fishery back in '62.

"It's an affront to our entire cultural preservation efforts," Mrs. Elefsson protests, calling for a town boycott.

As many of you know, the 128-year-old Olsson House, which originally resided in Green Bay, gained historical significance in the early 1900s when Olaf Olsson dragged it across the frozen lake by horses and deposited it at

Whitefish Creek's hilltop entrance at 1201 Main Street.

Svea Olsson-Vanderhoof, the niece who inherited the home after Olaf's death in 1963, made a statement from her Florida retirement community that it was time to sell. She said she gave the Door County Historical Society many years to raise the necessary funding to preserve it as a museum, and those efforts fell far short.

"I'm just glad somebody was willing to spend all the money needed on repairs before it collapsed," Ms. Olsson-Vanderhoof added.

Mo McKenna says she's already put a leprechaun trap outside her back door, so be on the lookout.

For those interested in catching their own leprechaun, Mo recommends building a contraption with a net, box, or anything you can think of (the more creative the better), and use a gold or silver coin for bait. She cautioned that no two traps should ever look alike, or leprechauns will get suspicious.

"They're clever little buggers," Mo says, but claims she's always had the best luck catching them on St. Patrick's Day (March 17th). "That's when they're the most careless. Because they're all pissed drunk."

Mrs. Elefsson wishes to remind everyone about the special Gibraltar Township meeting this Thursday night to discuss the Historical Society's proposed ordinance banning any flag displays on Main Street that are not Scandinavian or American.

CHAPTER 4

GOATS

Put silk on a goat and it's still a goat.

—Irish saying

MEG THOUGHT ABOUT TURNING AROUND several times on the cross-country journey. Or veering towards one of her brothers in Atlanta or Houston. Anything but rejoining her mother.

They were like two identical magnets. The closer Meg approached the stronger the resistance.

The instant Meg crossed into Wisconsin her stress level rose.

When she drove over the lone drawbridge that separated Wisconsin's northern peninsula from the rest of the world, the knot in her stomach tightened, while everything around her slowed down.

Fourteen years passed since she last stepped foot in Door County, and not a thing changed: its wildflower laden meadows; orchards of cherry trees; Swedish red barns (some experiencing new lives as artist galleries and antique shops); and all the Scandinavian flags interspersed with the Stars-and-Stripes.

This world seemed forever locked in the 1950s, with no big box stores, no McDonald's, no franchises of any kind. It was a place kids still rode bikes on dirt roads to the old-fashioned soda fountain for a root beer float on warm summer evenings.

The northern peninsula echoed with ghosts from Meg's past. It was their family's favorite summer vacation spot when their father was alive. And after his untimely death a day before Meg's 15th birthday, it became Meg's summer exile following the rebellious teen's arrest for organizing the biggest scavenger hunt their quaint St. Louis municipality of Kirkwood ever witnessed, resulting in the theft of traffic signs, manhole covers, and a police radar gun (a snatch Meg took full credit for). Meg's godmother Mary Lou Fitzgibbons whisked away the broken teenager for a quiet summer of mending at the Fitzgibbons' Door County beach house before blood hit the walls. And it still remained both the most magical and worst summer of Meg's life.

The thought of returning released an assault of suppressed feelings that she hoped some delicious Swedish pancakes and a well-needed beer at Door County's legendary Al Johnson's might help ease before jumping aboard her mother's train wreck.

When Meg turned up Sister Bay's main street—with the great lake on one side and its white clapboard shops on the other—she spotted the familiar sight of Al Johnson's famous goats grazing on the Swedish restaurant's sod-covered roof.

During the summer, tourists backed into one another, into cars, into traffic, smiling, waving, laughing, taking thousands of pictures of the famous rooftop goats. There were Lars, Nels, Olaf, and Jerk, whose fame to Door Countians and its tourists rivaled Mickey Mouse, Donald Duck, Minnie Mouse, and Goofy.

But Meg only counted three.

A fishing boat on the great lake's eastern horizon distracted Meg's attention, flooding her with memories of that summer, and she wondered if *he* might be aboard when something jumped in front of her car.

SLAM – !

Meg stomped the brakes. Her head snapped forward at impact. A dark thing bounced hard off the full of her Volkswagen Bug's grill.

Meg fumbled to open the car door. Her state of shock failed to register the large gash in her forehead where it smacked the windshield.

What she discovered stopped her breath.

It wasn't just a pedestrian she hit.

It was worse.

At the front of her car in the middle of the main street lay a goat.

Not just any goat. One of Al Johnson's world-famous goats.

"I'm so sorry," Meg apologized to the goat, unsure how to help the animal. She hedged towards it, and its body jerked, struggling to limp back on its unstable legs then crumpled.

A mob of concerned locals and tourists swarmed to the

animal's aid. Those staff members from Al Johnson's wore lederhosen, Swedish dresses, and wooden shoes. And all cast death glares at Meg.

"It's Lars!" a male voice shouted as they surrounded the goat.

"I'm so sorry," Meg felt horrible. "I couldn't have been going more than 10 or 15 miles an hour."

"Then how the hell'd ya hit him, ay!" an elder string-bean of a man snapped.

Meg felt nauseous. She ran over Door County's Mickey Mouse, and right there, in front of everyone, she doubled over and vomited—on the goat!

"Ahhhh!" the crowd gasped.

"Oh God," Meg choked as everything started to blur.

Then as she tried to stand upright to face the villagers' ire, her legs gave out and she collapsed.

CHAPTER 5

DEATH BY IRISHNESS

*In life, there are only two things to worry about—either you are
well or you are sick;*

*If you are well, there is nothing to worry about; but if you are sick,
there are only two things to worry about—either you will get well
or you will die;*

*If you get well, there is nothing to worry about; but if you die, there
are only two things to worry about—either you will go to heaven or
hell;*

*If you go to heaven, there is nothing to worry about; and if you go
to hell, you'll be so busy shaking hands with all your friends you
won't have time to worry!*

—an Irishman's philosophy

MEG AWOKE WITH A THROBBING headache, twelve
stitches in her forehead, and a soft Irish jig wafting from a
downstairs stereo that resonated like Chinese water torture.

She looked up from the worn couch in a fog. The living
space she now found herself consisted of a back bedroom,

tiny bath, a cozy family room where she now rested, and in the kitchenette, on the windowsill, she spotted her mother's white Madonna statuette (because her mother swore you'd never cut your finger in the kitchen with a Madonna).

She was above her mother's recently opened, half-baked Irish shop! Wrapped up on the couch in her great-grandmother's wool quilt with the stitched, ancient-Celtic, brail-like writing Ogham (pronounced *OH-yam*) that spelled something "profound" like: *You must take the little potato with the big potato.*

Meg felt like a fly wrapped in a spider's cocoon waiting to be eaten, as she anticipated her mother's assault of guilt trips and overbearing righteousness that promised to tear into her already low self-esteem.

Meg had suffered a concussion. But while Lars received celebrity medical attention, Meg sat in the ER fending off dirty looks from staff and patients until her mother Mo bailed her out.

Moira "Mo" (pronounced *Moe*) McKenna was a striking beauty at age 64. She had shoulder-length amber hair, pristine milky white skin, glowing smile and cheekbones, and by all accounts, was a well-bred feline with fiery Irish eyes and a dash of crazy.

Meg always felt her own looks paled in comparison to her mother and older sister. She was more a tomcat, with an eye for mischief and a penchant for rotten luck. Her mother swore she was born with a double-dose of original sin. And running over Door County's favorite son (or goat, as it were) couldn't have been more telling about what rotten luck lied ahead.

Meg felt sick about the goat. She wanted to check in on it, but the hospital staff and locals refused her request.

"I think you have your hands full just taking care of yourself," one of the locals dismissed her.

A stoic Mo McKenna walked into the ER's waiting room.

"The whole town's ready to take up torches and pitchforks," Mo addressed her estranged daughter.

"I thought you could use my help."

"So you go kill one of Al Johnson's goats?"

"It's still alive."

"Maybe. Which is more than you can say about that car of yours. 'Tis a miracle that thing made it across the country."

"What do you mean 'maybe' the goat's alive?"

"They took it to the animal hospital. This adds more ammunition for that witch Emmie Elefsson. We better pray that goat lives. Is it true you vomited on him?"

Meg slept the next few days, recovering from her concussion.

Once again, she closed her eyes and drifted back to sleep on her mother's couch, resigned to wakeup from this terrible dream when…"Amen! Amen! Amen!"

Mo stood over her like some crazy Irish shaman squeezing Meg's hand and tossing salt over her head.

"By the power of the Father, the Son, and the Holy Ghost, let me luv's brain heal, and the spell of evil spirits be broken! Amen! Amen! Amen!"

Meg yanked away from her mother's grasp and shooed her.

The next evening at supper, Meg found small strips of paper in her stew. "There's paper in here," Meg grimaced, picking another strip from her mouth.

"It helps you get better," her mother answered. "Oi wrote the name of Jaysus noine toimes and tore it up in the stew," she reassured Meg, as if the explanation made perfect sense. Her hard *i* sounded like *oi* with her dripping Irish tongue.

Her mother even reverted to her old childhood remedy of rubbing boiled potatoes on Meg's pained brow and then burying them in the backyard to cure headaches, which oddly enough worked most times.

"Enough with the crazies!" Meg shooed her off.

Her mother took offense. "'Tis the blessin' of the Virgin Mother I'm callin'."

"Then take that thing and rub it all over your shop. Maybe then you'll get a customer."

Mo stuck her tongue out ruefully at Meg—*plbbbbb*!

Pllbbbb—Meg stuck hers back at Mo. And Mo huffed downstairs with her potato.

Door County merchants banked 90% of their revenue from June to August. And Meg knew a lousy summer spelled certain bankruptcy for the shop her mother foolishly squandered her entire life's savings to open.

Their dear friend Mary Lou Fitzgibbons reported that the only paying customer since the shop's grand opening a month earlier consisted of an odd 60-ish-year-old man Mary Lou dubbed "Hat Guy," who apparently showed up each Friday to exchange the hat he picked the previous week for a new one. And the locals kept stealing her Irish flag out front and replacing it with a dead fish. Meg witnessed this herself, until an enraged Mo climbed a ladder onto the shop's grass-covered roof, shimmied up the tallest fir tree, and attached the biggest Irish flag in her arsenal.

"Let's see you steal that!" Mo shouted to the wind.

When Meg questioned the shop's dismal balance sheet, Mo dismissed any concerns with a wave of her hand. "The good Lord will provide."

But the good Lord wasn't shopping for Irish supplies, and as the critical summer season began, no one in Door County appeared to be either.

CHAPTER 6

THE DOOR COUNTIAN

Wisconsin's Largest Twice-Weekly Newspaper

Featured Columnist...
Seneca Parks

Goat Vigil

ON TUESDAY AFTERNOON, in front of Al Johnson's, a car struck our beloved Lars the goat. Lars apparently jumped off the roof moments before and wandered into the street. He suffered a broken hind leg and fractured ribs. Rescuers rushed him to Door County Memorial Hospital and later to the animal hospital in Sturgeon Bay. Doctors reported his condition as serious, but hopeful.

The Door County Historical Society plans to hold a candlelight vigil for Lars outside Al Johnson's this Friday night at 7 p.m.

The driver of the offending vehicle was 30-year-old Megan McKenna.

Eyewitnesses to the scene reported that after Ms.

McKenna struck Lars, she walked over and vomited on him.

Ms. McKenna's mother, Moira McKenna, recently opened the Irish store in Whitefish Creek.

CHAPTER 7

ACTING THE MAGGOT

acting the maggot—(vb. phr.) behaving in a humorously irrational manner

MEG AWOKE WITH A START.

The piercing sound split her brain.

Every afternoon since the concussion, the god-awful rattle clattered in her head like a crazed monkey banging a drum. It came from the north, growing louder, more excruciating, until it ripped her a migraine as it clattered past the shop. She even heard it late one night and awoke the next morning to find another dead fish hanging off their flagpole (although lately a series of homemade goats appeared on their lawn with the words "GOAT KILLER!").

Meg rushed outside to confront the offending vehicle in the middle of an empty Main Street like a gunslinger at high noon.

An old converted milk truck appeared from the trees. It was spray painted red and looked held together by twine. Deer antlers grew from the roof, a raccoon's tail hung from the rearview mirror, and on its side, painted in rudimentary penmanship (which looked like that of a six-year-old boy's), were the white letters: "Northern Lights Fish Co. Field Car."

The truck screeched to a stop a few feet from Meg.

A thousand needles tingled through her breathless body as the truck's door opened with a rusty pop and out stepped the ghost from that summer of her 16th year.

Robbie Knudson.

Robbie probably carried 20 more well-needed pounds. His face was rugged and mature, more handsome than she remembered. A small scar sliced his chin that wasn't there before. His weathered Norwegian blond locks whisked out of the same frayed, green ball cap he wore fourteen years ago. In fact, all his clothes appeared the same he wore fourteen years earlier: his silly coveralls; flannel shirt; hefty galoshes that thumped everywhere he walked; and the odor of fish.

"Meg?"

Meg felt butterflies. Thirty years old and her stomach fluttered like a giddy schoolgirl.

"What are you doing here?" Robbie asked with a smile that wanted to leap off his face. "Besides killing goats."

Meg stammered. Of course he knew. Everyone in this small town knew.

"I did not kill any goats! It jumped in front of me. There was nothing I could do!"

"Except vomit on him," Robbie chuckled.

"I had a concussion," Meg insisted. "Stop laughing. I feel bad enough as it is."

"You really are unlucky, aren't you," Robbie recalled

with a smile. "I didn't think you could make folks around here hate you more than starting an Irish shop. But hitting one of Al Johnson's goats. Way to raise the bar."

"You probably shouldn't be talking with the enemy then," Meg said.

"That's a pretty good scar on your forehead," Robbie pointed to her stitches.

"Just fix your truck," Meg snapped. "I can hear it a mile away!"

"A mile?" Robbie grinned skeptically.

"Out my window," Meg pointed to the dormer, and to her shock, noticed not only the absence of the shop's Irish flag, but in its place, from the fir tree atop their sod covered roof, flew a bright red Norwegian flag with its blue and white cross.

They'd been recolonized!

Robbie chuckled. "I like your flag."

"You did that!" Meg accused him. "You've been the one stealing our flag and hanging dead fish on the flag pole, haven't you?"

Robbie chuckled, his open hands claiming innocence.

"I know you too well, Robbie Knudson."

"Now wait a second. I did not do that. I maybe hung one dead fish."

Meg didn't buy it.

"Maybe two," Robbie conceded.

Meg's amber brow raised.

"And a goat. But that's it."

Down Main Street, Meg glimpsed Emmie Elefsson staring up from her store's front porch with a big, gloating grin.

Meg fumed. "Just fix your truck!" she blurted and rushed back to the shop, trying to make sense out of what just happened, or more accurately, stomp out any inconvenient feelings.

Mo startled her as she stopped inside the shop's doorway. "You look like you saw a ghost."

Mo spied out the window at the departing truck. "Do you know him?"

Meg still felt polarized. Then something triggered inside her. Perhaps retribution for his truck. Or maybe pent up frustration from 14 years ago. Whatever its origin, her horns popped out.

When Robbie traipsed back to his truck after delivering a full tub of fish to the Whitefish Creek Grill all his tires were as flat as Swedish pancakes.

Robbie looked around for the vandal, recognizing the handy work all too well.

Meg!

CHAPTER 8

THE WATER OF LIFE

Dance as if no one's watching,
sing as if no one's listening,
and live each day as if it were your last.

—*Irish proverb*

MEG LAUGHED ABOUT THE first time she met Robbie
Knudson. It was the summer of her 16th birthday. He walked
up to the Fitzgibbons's beach house with his nest of blond
hair, soiled brown coveralls, ratty plaid shirt, a big steel tub
of fish, and a pack of tail-wagging dogs jumping all over him
as he struggled to shake them off his overwhelming fish
odor. "Shoo!"

It was the first time Meg laughed since her father's death
a year earlier.

Meg recalled commenting he needed to be power
washed. Robbie called her a tourist. And when she protested,
Robbie challenged her to prove otherwise by eating half a
pound of some pre-cooked, favorite local Scandinavian fish

delicacy called lutefisk (which, when he unwrapped one from his tub, looked like gray, snot-like goo).

Meg gagged down about half before darting for the closest bathroom. She spent the next 12 hours attached to the toilet like a barnacle, cursing Robbie's name, while Mary Lou, in a thick B*ah*ston accent that four decades of Midwestern living failed to dilute, informed her that the literal translation of lutefisk was "two-week old rotten cod soaked in plutonium." But plutonium wasn't harsh enough for the Vikings, so they soaked it in lye. "I wouldn't let the g*aw*ddamn dog eat that," Mary Lou exclaimed, with all her hard o's and r's sounded like *ah*.

"He called me a tourist," Meg seethed. "I couldn't let him win."

"Darling, there's no gawddamn place in this world where eating <u>that</u> is winning." Mary Lou was a tall, thin, dark-curly-haired New England grand dame who dressed like a socialite and cussed like a sailor. "I'm telling you, if you can still taste the difference between caviar and crap, you're not drunk enough to eat that shit."

The next morning, Robbie clomped down the wooden dock at dawn and heard the laughter of other fishermen as he saw an entire colony of gulls squatting in his 17-foot skiff, with every inch of his boat caked in excrement.

"Cripes!" he said in disgust, throwing down his netting and tackle and scaring them off. Then he noticed remnants of birdseed interspersed with pieces of Ex-Lax.

He'd been sabotaged!

Later that day, Meg answered the Fitzgibbons' screen door to find Robbie standing on the porch with two small fish in his large tub.

"I thought I'd give you the honor of buying the only two fish I caught all day—seeing that you were the evil genius behind it all."

"That's all you caught?"

"That's what happens when you get a late start because you have to scrub an inch-thick layer of bird shit out your boat. Excuse my language."

Meg chuckled.

"Sure, laugh," Robbie fumed. "All fun and games. Easy lazy summer for you tourists. But some of us have to work. I have a mom and five younger brothers to support. And that late start cost me a day's pay."

Meg didn't realize. "I'm sorry," she said, feeling guilty. "Can I make it up to you?"

"You have two hundred and four dollars?" Robbie doubted. "Cause that's what I'm short today."

"How about I help you catch twice as much tomorrow to make up for it."

"Ha! The only help I need is someone who can work nets and gut fish. I don't need some squeamish *tourist*."

Robbie marched out the gate where a couple of excited dogs waited to jump all over him. "Shoo!" he said, protecting his two fish.

Calling Meg a *tourist* riled her, but Robbie's mention of losing a father prompted Meg to arise before dawn the next morning and appear on the docks wearing old jeans, a sweatshirt, and Mary Lou's thickest garden gloves. "Ready to gut fish," she said boldly as she climbed into his boat.

A surprised Robbie shook off his better judgment. "I'm

gonna regret this…"

The next eight hours Meg suffered through the hazing of setting nets, hoisting and untangling oily fish (some wriggling out of her hands to Robbie's exasperation), but the grittiness she showed mucking through the fish slime and guts earned Robbie's respect.

"Hey," Robbie called Meg as she headed home after a solid day's work. "I pay deckhands eight bucks an hour if you're interested. I shove off at the crack of dawn, with or without you."

"Tell me one thing. Honestly. Did you find my prank funny?"

Robbie's brows crunched. "You turned my boat into an outhouse!"

"Did you laugh a little bit?"

It pained Robbie to admit. "A little."

Meg grinned. "See you tomorrow then."

Meg appeared the next morning. And almost every morning thereafter.

They laughed a lot those days. Teasing one another on the high seas and talking for hours. Robbie told her how he too lost his father at an early age. Now almost 18, Robbie spent the last five years caring for his mother and five younger siblings, skipping school, and eventually becoming a full-time fisherman with dreams of one day owning his own rig. Meg told Robbie about her big, crazy Irish family and the vast hole her father left, along with her penchant for bad Irish luck.

The two became inseparable. Meg rose early most mornings, and Robbie taught her to lay nets, gut fish, and showed her the secrets of Door County. Meg taught him how to dance an Irish jig and spin tall tales like a real *shanachie* (Irish storyteller). They even encountered Door County's last remaining lighthouse keeper (an odd hermit the locals called Alewife Alma), who tried to con them into buying her rotten alewife (which Meg learned were fish). And one unseasonably cold July 4th night, they kissed for the first time, and wondered why they waited so long. Perhaps they feared jeopardizing a friendship they both cherished. Or perhaps that free fall of love scared them.

Robbie took Meg to his family's cherry orchard the following week to meet his five brothers and mother. And Meg never forgot the deep sadness in Svea Knudson's eyes.

"She never learned to let go of my father," Robbie later lamented, confiding in Meg how she still struggled with depression that sometimes left her bedridden for weeks.

The next afternoon, as they sat docked near one of Door County's 11 old lighthouses, Robbie caught Meg doodling dress designs with grease pens and newspaper she found in his boat; and she told him about the time she made a dress for a lonely old neighbor. "It made her really happy," Meg smiled. "I always thought that would be fun. Designing clothes that make people feel good. I thought I'd make one for your mom." She showed her sketch as they shared a heartfelt smile.

As July approached August, one warm, star-filled night they snuck into Lighthouse Island's haunted tower.

"Its keeper disappeared at sea in the late 1800s," Robbie said. "On dark nights, people say you can sometimes see his widow's ghost in the light tower still looking for his return,"

Robbie grinned. And in this romantic beacon of a time long past, they lost their virginity.

What Meg later recalled about both their first time was that it hurt, and it lasted all of a minute, but sharing the whole out-of-body intensity with Robbie was a moment she wanted to stay in forever.

Robbie's memory of that magical night differed.

It came crashing down when he returned home and found his mother curled in a lifeless fetal position on the living room floor with an empty bottle of sleeping pills.

A horrified Robbie jumped to her. No pulse. He tried frantic CPR. Shouted to his five sleeping siblings to call 911.

She left no suicide note. No goodbye. Svea Knudson abandoned them without a word.

A week after his mother's funeral, Robbie coldly announced that his new responsibilities to raise his five younger siblings left no time to waste goofing around with her. Meg knew Robbie blamed himself for his mother's death, and no matter how far she reached out to help, it only made things worse.

"I should've been with her," he cursed their magical night on Lighthouse Island. "That was a mistake."

And that was the last thing he said before Meg's inner-Irishman exploded his face with a punch to the snot locker and she ran off upset.

Robbie never came after her. And Meg eventually moved on.

CHAPTER 9

SHENANIGANS

A good laugh and a long sleep are the best cures
in a doctor's book.

—*Irish proverb*

AFTER HER UNEXPECTED RUN-IN with Robbie, Meg lay awake thinking about that long-ago summer in Door County. It felt like no time passed as she drifted back 14 years, then CRASH! Something metal struck the side of the house, followed by shouts in the street with Mo's brogue leading the charge.

"Let's see you steal me flag now!" Mo shouted.

Meg glanced outside to discover a steel ladder under her window with her crazed mother flecked with orange and green paint, standing in the front yard, and the entire shop painted one enormous, billboard-sized Irish flag! Three huge orange-white-and-green tri-stripes covered the shop's front exterior wall like some gaudy roadside attraction.

"That monstrosity will only make your shop die a quicker death," Emmie Elefsson shouted up from her

Whitefish Creek Mercantile, a few blocks down. The 50-something Nordic blond beauty stood on her store's wraparound cedar porch that boasted an embassy of Norwegian flags and two giant wooden Nordic troll statues. "I already have a black dress picked out for its funeral!" she smirked.

"Well I'll show up wearin' red at yours! That's more appropriate where yer goin'!"

Emmie dismissed Mo with a backhand, and marched inside, punctuating her disapproval with a screen door slam.

Mo smiled and kept on painting.

The next week, Robbie continued to clatter into Whitefish Creek with his wretched rattletrap truck. Every afternoon as he drove past the shop, Meg suffered a splitting migraine. And every afternoon Robbie walked out of the Whitefish Creek Grill he found his tires flat.

"Dang it!" He said after the third time.

On the fourth day, Robbie glued down his tires' air caps, thwarting Meg's daily sabotage.

The following afternoon, Robbie confidently parked at the Whitefish Creek Grill and took his sweet old time delivering fish—enough time to let Meg jump from the bushes and dump an enormous bag of birdseed (and Ex-Lax chunks) over the offending vehicle. When Robbie emerged, some 40 seagulls squatted over every inch of his truck.

"Shoo!" he swiped at the defiant creatures until they flapped off to reveal his entire truck caked in bird droppings.

"That's real original!" he shouted for Meg to hear, stomping into his truck, unable to see out his gray-covered windshield. He then flicked on the wiper fluid to watch black grease shoot all over.

Meg! He cursed, and then laughed at her brinkmanship.

When Robbie's truck failed to appear the next day, Meg dozed off victoriously to Door County's outdoor lullaby of lapping waves and woodland creatures that breezed through her open window.

Somewhere during the middle of the night, a cherry flew through the open window and rolled on the floor. Another soared through and landed on her couch. Then another and another and another...

The next morning, Meg awoke from a great slumber. She rubbed her eyes. Blinked several times. And as the room came into focus, hundreds of skinny winged bugs covered the ceiling and her.

Meg screamed as she leapt off the couch into this swarm. Cherries squished under her bare feet as she raced downstairs, fighting and spitting away the bugs.

"Well look who's up," Mo glanced over from the counter, where she and Mary Lou sipped fresh-brewed Barry's Irish Tea, only to drop their jaws in horror at the sight of this Egyptian plague buzzing downstairs. "Jaysus, Mary and Joseph!"

Pestilence flooded the main store, and Meg, Mary Lou, and Mo fled outside.

"They were all over the ceiling!" Meg spit the taste of bugs from her mouth. "Didn't you see them when you woke up?"

"I didn't look at the ceilin'," Mo said. "What are they?"

"Cherry bugs," Mary Lou said. "They like fruit. Anything sweet. We got them all the time if we left out windows open after cherry picking."

"Cherries," Meg now knew the culprit.

"Good morning," a friendly man in a suit interrupted.

"How is yerself?" Mo beamed at the sight of an actual customer.

"Moira McKenna?" the man smiled.

"'Tis me," she grinned.

The man handed her papers. "Normally we send this certified mail, but since there hasn't been postal delivery in Whitefish Creek for twenty years, you get special service."

"What's this?" she smiled.

"A notice from the bank," he smiled cordially. "It looks like you're several months behind in your mortgage."

Mo looked at the letter and saw the words "..foreclosure if not current."

"The summer season's just startin'," Mo shot up. "We'll catch up."

"I'm just the messenger. You need to call Fordel Hogenson at the bank if you want to avoid immediate foreclosure."

"I don't have this kind of money right now."

"I'm sorry. Have a nice day."

CHAPTER 10

POT O' GOLD

If you do not sow in the spring,
you will not reap in the fall.

—*Irish proverb*

"DRESS LIKE WHAT?" Mo protested. "I will in me hat!"

"I know it's a little corny – "

"'Tis Plastic Paddyism, 'tis what 'tis!"

"If we don't generate revenue fast, you'll be foreclosed on. Look. I sewed us jackets and ordered these hats. Red. See."

Mo loathed the Hallmark version of green dim-witted leprechauns, smoking pipes, and affably sitting on pots of gold under a rainbow. Real leprechauns wore red: red coat, red cocked hat, red shoes. They were cobblers. Nothing to do with pots of gold (other than to steal someone else's), and were mischievous little buggers with foul tempers who'd piss on a rainbow if given the chance.

"This is the big summer kickoff. If you can't win over

the tourists, this shop is sunk. Look. I even sewed seven rows of seven gold buttons on the jackets," Meg emphasized a detail Mo always preached about leprechauns as she waited for the slightest glimmer of enthusiasm.

"I will not let me shop's reputation be tarnished by shameless panderin'."

"What reputation?" Meg shot. "Everyone hates us!"

"God has a plan," Mo reassured herself.

"Does His plan involve paying the mortgage anytime soon?"

"'Tis always instant gratification wid yer generation. God's not Google. 'Tis a lot of people's needs He has to coordinate. But I've niver been more certain that this place, right here, is exactly where I need to be, and exactly what I need to be doin' at this very moment. When have you ever been able to say that about anythin'?"

Meg failed to recall such a time in her floundering life, other than perhaps that summer in Door County.

SCREECH.

The outside sound jerked Meg and Mo towards the window. A truck pulled up with a bobcat. Enormous 20-feet-tall fir trees protruded from its bed. They watched three men hop out, then lower the bobcat onto the shop's front sidewalk. When the bobcat dropped its shovel and plowed into the strip of grass between the sidewalk and street, Mo and Meg stormed outside.

"What in the bejaysus are you doin'?" Mo exclaimed to the men. "This is me property! Stop this instant!"

"That's your property," he pointed towards the shop's side of the walk. "That's the town's," he pointed to the strip the bobcat ripped into. "We got an order from the city to plant five pines right here."

"Those pines are huge," Meg protested. "You can't do that. No one will be able to see the shop!"

"Talk to City Council," the man handed Mo the invoice. Councilwoman Emmie Elefsson signed the authorization.

Mo already suspected Emmie encouraged the bank to foreclose. And as her Irish temper boiled, Mo stormed two blocks down Main Street to Emmie's Whitefish Creek Mercantile. It was twice the size of Mo's shop, sickeningly adorable, filled with perfect Scandinavian and Door County merchandise, and even more sobering, packed with customers.

"Emmie Elefsson," Mo shouted through the crowd of patrons. "You won't get away with this!"

Emmie smiled confidently, her prized black lab Flowers at her feet. "So nice of you and your goat-killing daughter to visit my shop."

Mo jumped in her face. "If you think I'm goin' to sit by and let you hide me shop with those trees, you got another thing comin'."

Emmie smiled sweetly for the sake of her watchful customers. "No one wants you or your ridiculous shop here."

Mo stared her square in the eye. "I'd rather be absolutely ridiculous than absolutely boring."

Emmie looked annoyed, but forced a smile to keep face as Mo took her leave.

"Incidentally," Emmie called to her. "If you're thinking

about cutting any of those newly planted trees down, each infraction carries a maximum fine of five hundred dollars and sixty days in jail. And I know the judge would be happy to enforce that."

Mo's eyes cursed her. "May you be afflicted with a desperate itch and have no nails to scratch with!"

Mo stormed out with Meg in tow as everyone in the store chuckled.

CHAPTER 11

FYR BAL

Red hot embers are easily rekindled.

—Irish proverb

A COLD GRAY DRIZZLE kept away the Fyr Bal Festival's anticipated throng of tourists from Ephraim's thin, half-moon stretch of mile-long beach where an intermittent line of towering, unlit bonfires grew wetter by the hour. The watered-down smell of brats, waffle cones, and Swedish pastries enticed a sparse umbrella-toting crowd of locals and hard-core summer residents, many dressed in traditional Norwegian sweaters or Viking helmets, waving small Norwegian flags, as they awaited Door County's most celebrated tradition—the summer's first official fish boil, which preceded the lighting of the bonfires and the anxiously-awaited revelation of this year's esteemed Fyr Bal Chieftain. The Chieftain arrived off the lake at dusk on a ceremonial Viking ship, crowned with the traditional Vikinghorned helmet and adorned in a red cape. The high honor was Door County's equivalent to Citizen of the Year. And the Fyr Bal Committee's confidential selection process provided healthy debate throughout the slow winter months as to the coming year's nomination.

Meg spent the day in her red leprechaun jacket and hat distributing a bag of half-dollar-size promotional gold coins she secretly ordered with the few hundred dollars she made selling her dead car for parts. The front inscription read ALL THINGS IRISH SHOP, and the back said $1 STORE CREDIT. People threw them in her face, discarded them in the trash, spit on them, and a good many people walked away uttering a contemptuous "goat killer."

"You should try serving beer," Robbie called to her.

Robbie's *Northern Lights Fishing Company* truck rested along the shoreline road about ten meters from an old Speed Queen washing tub that hung off a pole structure assembled at the edge of the beach over a large stack of burning logs. A crowd amassed around this season's first fish boil, while Robbie—the master fish boiler—rummaged through the back of his truck for the final ingredients.

"We're not a pub," Meg said as she walked over, offended by this stereotype.

"This is Wisconsin," Robbie smiled as Meg neared. "You want to win friends, do what you Irish do best."

Robbie climbed out the back of the truck with a large old coffee can filled with kerosene.

"Please tell me you're not dumping that on the fish?"

"It's not lutefisk season yet," Robbie grinned, and their smiling eyes met full on in a stomach-jumping free fall.

"Megan McKenna!" Mo's angry voice broke the moment.

Meg glimpsed Mo fast approaching through the crowd.

"Shit!" Meg tossed the contraband coins behind Robbie.

Mo glared at the red leprechaun outfit as if Meg committed high treason.

"I thought we agreed not to dress up today," Mo gritted out a smile, the place too public to make a scene. Then she took notice of Robbie. "I'm Moira McKenna," she flashed a charming smile and extended her hand. "Meg's mother. But everyone calls me Mo."

"Robbie Knudson," Robbie shook her hand. "Nice to finally meet you."

"Finally?" Mo said suspect.

"Meg's told me a lot about you."

"When might that have been?" Mo smiled suspiciously.

"Well, I guess, most from way back."

"Mo, who's attending the shop?" Meg tried to change subjects.

"'Tis locked," Mo said, awaiting an answer. "So how far back?"

"Summer long time ago. Back when we used to fish on my outboard — "

"The summer you spent at Mary Lou's," Mo cocked her brow like a gun, then, as if a light went off, she turned the barrel on Robbie. "Did you flah me daughter?"

"Mother!" Meg demanded she stop.

"Did you shag her?" Mo pressed. "Have sex with her?"

Robbie appeared taken aback.

"Mother!" Meg cautioned.

The fish boil's crowd took notice of their rising temperaments.

Mo stuck her right index finger like a loaded Derringer in Robbie's surprised face. "You have no idea what you did," she seethed at Robbie. "No idea!"

"Then why don't you tell him?" Meg urged.

"I'm goin' back to the shop," Mo marched away in a fury.

Meg's hand slapped around Mo's wrist like handcuffs and Mo spun around, shocked. "Why won't you say it? Fourteen years you've acted like it never happened. I want to hear you say it."

"You're makin' a holy show of yerself." Mo tempered her tone to defuse the onlookers' attention. "'Tis not the time or place."

"Are you still so ashamed of it after fourteen years?"

Mo raised a perceptive brow. "Are you?"

The words proved a harsh mirror Meg was unprepared to gaze upon as Mo yanked free her arm, leaving Meg to wallow in her last comment.

"Alright," Robbie tried to distract the audience by grabbing his coffee can of kerosene to ignite the fire in the fish boil's much-anticipated grand finale explosion. "Everyone stand back or you're liable to get your hair shortened."

"Say it!" Something triggered inside Meg as Mo walked away. "Do you hear me? I want you to say it. He's the one who got me pregnant!"

Mo froze.

The crowd froze.

Robbie froze.

The kerosene Robbie just tossed onto the fire did not.

Pfooom — *!* Flames blasted around a stunned Robbie. His hair caught fire. He rushed into the bay, swatting at his smoldering locks as he splashed into the lake.

Meg covered her gaping mouth as Robbie emerged with a red scalp and singed hair.

Mo shook her head at his idiocy and stormed off.

A shell-shocked Robbie stared up at Meg, entire patches of hair missing from his burnt scalp as he searched her eyes for answers she wasn't ready to give.

A few people came to his aid, imploring him to go to the ER, but Robbie focused on a distraught Meg who retreated into the crowd.

CHAPTER 12

SAINT BRIGID'S

May the angels of heaven be among us,
may the friends of heaven be gathered around us,
may there be a great lake of beer for the King of Kings,
and may heaven's family drink it through all eternity.

—*Saint Brigid of Ireland*

ROBBIE CHASED MEG. He said nothing as he caught up to her, walking patiently amidst the bonfires as Meg worked through the pain of unearthing the memory. They walked half a mile down the beach before she spoke.

"It's just something that happened," she tried to brush it aside.

Meg knew abortion was out of the question. She was too young to become a single mother. And by no means wanted to become a 16-year-old bride trapped in Door County the rest of her life, which was exactly what Robbie's duty-bound conscience would insist happen if he found out.

Meg knew if she let Mo raise the child, her mother

would hold it over her head until the end of days. Which left adoption the only acceptable solution. And Mo insisted it couldn't be just any adoption. It had to be an adoption to a good Catholic family. At least that ensured the baby received a proper baptism.

Meg called in her sister Caitlyn from Notre Dame to stand by her side when she dropped the bomb on Mo.

When Meg refused to divulge the father's identity, Mo made it clear never to speak of this again. If Meg suffered at all, Mo expected her to do so in silence, so as not to make the family feel "uncomfortable" for her sins. That was the Irish way. Then Mo forced Meg to talk to a priest. And since Meg's all-girl Catholic school refused to allow pregnant students, Mo took a page from a 1950s playbook on how to hide teen pregnancy and shipped Meg to an Irish nunnery that specialized in expectant teen mothers.

When Meg boarded the plane for Dublin, Mo startled her with an absorbing hug that seemed determined to protect Meg from all the world's cruelties. It was the longest embrace Meg ever received from her mother (certainly since her father's death). And when Mo finally let go, Meg did not want it to end.

"Use this," Mo's voice cracked, as she handed Meg a wooden rosary with the image of the Blessed Virgin carved in the cross of St. Brigid. "She'll help you if you ask for it," Mo said, referring to the Blessed Mother. "You just need to ask."

"Please, mother!" Meg thrust it back into Mo's resistant hands, tired of her constant religious appeals, and saw the heartbreak in Mo's eyes.

Somewhere over the Atlantic a cold tear rolled off Meg's cheek, wishing she had accepted the stupid rosary.

Meg spent the next six months rebelling against her captor's strict regimen of mass, chores, studies, prayer time (presumably to repent for their sins), and lights out by nine. The letters Meg received from her mother never once inquired about the pregnancy, and always ended with a plea to attend weekly confession. Mary Lou's notes kept her abreast of gossip and Mo's latest act of craziness (like refusing to throw away a bad bottle of wine without first dumping its contents because she feared winos would rummage through her garbage). But Meg really looked forward to her sister's letters. Caitlyn always asked about the pregnancy, if Meg felt the baby kicking, if she experienced any weird cravings, etc. Those letters sustained her as the due date drew frighteningly close. The sisters wrote every day, and Caitlyn revealed Mo's doubts about sending Meg away. Meg wrote back: "If she wants me back, she can ask," in a stubbornness to match her mother's. And Meg suppressed her secret hope of hearing from Robbie.

As the days and weeks passed, Meg watched her belly grow, turning her restless energy to sabotaging her captors. For starters, she wrapped the chapel bell in towels rendering its wretched pre-dawn wakeup call impotent. She walked naked through the halls, pregnant belly and all, to shock the prudish virgin brides of Christ. She flabbergasted her religious captors at mealtime by openly questioning whether Mary remained a virgin after she bore Jesus. But the worst came when she padlocked the sisters inside the chapel during 6:00 a.m. prayer service, swiped Mother Superior's car, and drove 80 miles to catch one of Ireland's biggest all-day music festivals—dressed as a pregnant nun no less.

When the nuns marched Meg into Mother Superior's stark office upon her return, the beautiful septuagenarian sat surprisingly calm as she stared silently at Meg. Meg endured about forty seconds of the uncomfortable silence before she cracked: "So are you going to kick me out or what?"

"I find it very telling of a person's character how they react to silence," she stared through Meg, making Meg shift uneasily. "Girls cope with unexpected pregnancies in different ways. The headstrong fight it 'til the bitter end. They try to maintain some kind of control over their lives by rebelling against it. But no matter how much you rebel, that baby is comin' whether you're ready or not."

The distinguished nun opened a gold locket revealing an old black-and-white photo of a newborn baby. "His name is Padraig," Mother Superior lovingly divulged. "He's me son."

Meg practically hit the floor in shock.

"Well I wasn't born a nun," Mother Superior said indignantly.

She proceeded to tell Meg about growing up dirt poor in Belfast. How she became pregnant at 14 and her family disowned her. She was five months along, living on the streets, until a nun took her in. She gave her child up for adoption and eventually joined the order, dedicating her life to providing a place for young girls pregnant out of wedlock and a hospital for the poor.

"If I niver got pregnant and wound up on the street, I niver would have helped all the girls who have come through these doors," she said softly. "Hardships are blessings in disguise—if you're willing to relinquish control and trust in God's higher plan. We cannot possibly know what lies ahead. Or always what is best for us. All we can do is help those we can and do the best with the circumstances we're given. 'Tis all for a reason. One day I hope you understand this."

In the weeks that followed, Meg grew more reflective about what lied ahead and what possible reason this bad Irish luck held.

Meg watched girls disappear for a few days to give birth and every time they returned to pack their things, they put on smiles and said little of the experience. Their eyes looked ten years older. Their spirits seemed broken and glued back together. One girl Meg befriended offered a final heartfelt word after returning from the hospital: "Don't let yourself get attached."

Meg was four weeks from delivery and frightened she too would never be the same.

A week later, Meg felt the worst pain of her life. It felt like someone took a shotgun and blew off her va-hoo-hoo. She saw blood in her broken water. Nuns rushed her to the O.R. where a team of concerned nurses hooked her to monitors and placed her legs in stirrups. No time for an epidural, Meg screamed from the ripping pain and confusion. They ordered her on her side. Something about the cord wrapped around the baby's neck. And Meg remembered crying out for her mother.

When Meg returned home after her six-month exile, Mo acted as if she just came back from a sleepover. No fanfare. No acknowledgment. Mo served leftovers for dinner, and made it very clear the matter was best left forgotten and never spoken of again.

"Was the baby okay?" Robbie asked.

Silence settled between them until Meg uttered "I don't know."

"What do you mean?"

"I didn't ask," Meg admitted with a tear. "I didn't want to know, okay? I didn't want to know anything about it."

Meg took a few more steps before realizing Robbie stopped.

"Don't judge me. You weren't there. You have no idea what I went through."

"You never gave me that chance." Robbie gazed over the lake with his heavy thoughts.

The distant lights of a freighter crept across the twilight.

"Was it a boy or a girl?" Robbie finally spoke.

Meg didn't answer.

"Was it a boy or girl?"

"I never asked," Meg said painfully.

Robbie turned without looking at her. "I need to go. I'm sorry." And he walked away.

CHAPTER 13

HOT POTATOES

You must take the little potato with the big potato.

—*Irish saying*

DOOR COUNTY'S GOSSIP VINES buzzed about Meg and Robbie's long-lost lovechild.

Meg wisely holed up at Mary Lou's to let Mo's Irish temper cool off after Meg's unforgivable public airing of family secrets.

"She still won't acknowledge I was ever pregnant," Meg complained to Mary Lou. "She's such a hypocrite. Do you know how much her whack job parenting messed me up over the years?"

"Darling, you know I love you like a daughter. But the whole 'child scorned' thing doesn't play past thirty. You can't blame your parents forever. There's a statute of limitations."

Meg sat speechless. "I thought you were on my side."

"Darling, we all have our crosses to bear. Lord knows Grace is mine," Mary Lou referred to her 18-year-old adopted daughter. "She brought home a possum the other day. A possum! As a pet! Meanest animal I've ever seen. It tore apart the house. The couch in our family room. Ripped it up and shat all over it. Now she has it in a pen out back and branded it with permanent marker. Put a big G on it. The girl is crazy."

"My mother's crazy."

"Life's more fun when your crazy," Mary Lou smiled. "Now your mother—you want to talk hard knocks—that woman grew up in a tiny two-bedroom shoebox with five younger siblings and was lucky to have one meal a day. Her father was a drunk. Her mother was bipolar. All your mother's friends were pregnant by sixteen. Her parents wanted her to quit high school and help support the family," Mary Lou divulged. "When she told her parents she planned to go to college, her mother threw her out the house for being all uppity. That's when your mother went into the convent — "

"Mo was in a convent?! She never told us that!"

"At that St. Brigid's. The place she shipped you. She thought the world of that mother superior there."

For the first time Meg saw the thought process in her mother's 1950s playbook.

"She would've become a nun if she hadn't met your father."

"What?" Meg couldn't believe it. "They said they met at school. Right after dad left the seminary and took a semester abroad."

Mary Lou laughed. "Your father was a visiting priest at the hospital. He broke his vows to marry your mother."

"No way!" Meg laughed. "I love it. Mo a harlot," Meg grinned, seeing her devout mother in a refreshing new light.

"Darling, life's not about your grand plan," Mary Lou said. "You have to be open to the signs and figure where life's guiding you. And if something seems inconvenient and scary, that's usually the right way."

"It doesn't matter," Meg dismissed it all. "The bank will kick us out soon."

"What did they say?" Mary Lou asked.

"She has to get current or they'll foreclose."

"I'm sure Emmie Elefsson has a hand in this," Mary Lou correctly surmised, as the wheels in her devilish head turned to find a solution—or a way to retaliate.

CHAPTER 14

ALEWIFE ALMA

If you don't want flour on your clothes, stay out of the mill.

—*Irish saying*

AFTER A WEEK OF ROBBIE ignoring Meg's calls, Meg marched to the docks before dawn, climbed into his large fishing tug named *The Osprey*, and refused to remove herself until they went fishing.

Rather than lose a day's catch, Robbie begrudgingly shook his head and revved the engine.

Meg was the most incorrigible person he ever met.

Neither spoke of the baby. In fact, Robbie refused to talk much about anything. So Meg worked quietly alongside him, slaving over the nets and fish, and enjoying the simple comfort of his presence.

"Where are we going?" Meg asked at the end of the day as they veered towards an island.

"Alewife Alma's. Thought I'd bring her some of our catch."

"Alewife Alma?" Meg said. "The woman who tried to

sell us rotten fish?"

"Makes for good lutefisk," Robbie smiled as they trolled up to the ramshackle pier.

The island appeared overgrown and rundown. A dozen or so stray cats milled around the 200-acre wooded island as they walked towards the lighthouse.

They passed a dilapidated barn and found Alma's thick, squat frame sitting on a wooden chair with a fishing pole cast into the woods.

"Alma?" Robbie flashed a peculiar grin. "What ya doin'?"

"Ay?" Alma said, the victim of a faulty hearing aid.

"What ya fishin' for?"

"Squirrels," Alma's eyes remained on the woods. "Damn things are too finicky. I got good peanut butter on the end there. All they want is macadamia nuts." Shouts into the woods: "Regal bastards!"

"I brought some fish for ya," Robbie set down a large tub of fish. "Where's old Buddy?" Robbie looked around for his favorite mutt.

"I took a gun to him last night."

Meg covered her mouth as she made a horrified gasp and Alma's head pivoted towards Meg.

"This here's Meg," Robbie introduced her. "She was helpin' me out on the boat today."

Alma's dark beady eyes fixated on Meg with deep scrutiny.

"Sorry to hear about Buddy," Robbie tried to distract Alma's glare. "He was a good old dog. Just got too sick, ay?"

"Got into another hornets' nest again," Alma said, her

dark eyes not letting go of Meg. "I told him last time he came home with a mouthful of stingers that I was too old to be pullin' 'em out with pliers. I said, 'If you don't have the God-given sense to leave hornets' nests alone, I'm gonna take a gun to ya'."

Alma was as odd a duck as ever flew in from the rain.

"You was right about her being pretty," Alma turned to Robbie.

"What?" Robbie questioned.

"Ain't she the Meg from that summer? The one you always said was the prettiest girl you ever saw?"

"What was that?" Meg asked Robbie with a raised brow.

"She's hard of hearing," Robbie grinned. "She doesn't know what she's talking about."

"Back when I used to come to your house," Alma called Robbie out.

"Alma used to help me with my brothers after my mom died."

"And you said she was the prettiest girl you ever saw."

Robbie fumbled over his tongue. "I don't quite recall what exactly I said back then..."

Meg enjoyed watching Robbie squirm.

"You said it a couple times," Alma insisted.

Robbie felt Meg's eyes upon him as she grinned.

"I was in a very aggrieved state. I don't remember," he glanced at Meg. "She's senile."

"He never brings people here," Alma noted.

Now Robbie seemed embarrassed. Meg glanced at him and smiled, nudging him playfully in the ribs.

Robbie lightheartedly discredited Alma's comment. "Her

mind's losing it."

Meg didn't buy a word.

"He always works," Alma said in her flat tone. "He's worked since he was a youngster. Don't know nothin' better. If he ain't fishin', he's workin' on his winery or the fish processin' plant. That Anna is just as bad. He has fun with you though." Alma stood. "I just finished distillin' a new batch of whiskey. Bring that fish inside and I'll pour us a glass. Robbie says you're Irish."

Many glasses later, the two inebriates stumbled back to the boat (completely "legless" as Mo would say), laughing and joking, with Alma's mention of some girl named Anna drowned in Meg's memory of booze.

"I want to know what Alma put in her whiskey," Meg said as they pulled away from the island.

"I don't know, but I'm pretty sure it can power this boat."

Meg's and Robbie's eyes held each other in a warm smile as they stood in the tug's small wheelhouse.

"So you don't bring people there?" Meg teased him.

"I usually stop by when I'm heading back from fishing. I like to check in a few times a week."

Meg smiled at Robbie. He was a good man.

"Sounds like you've done well for yourself," Meg said. "You got your fishing boat. A processing plant. A successful winery?"

"We converted the old orchard about ten years ago."

"It's your own little empire. Everything you ever wanted, you made happen."

"You think so, huh?" Robbie challenged her.

"It's perfect."

"Perfect," Robbie laughed at the word.

"What?"

"The last thing I want is perfect. Look at the sky." Robbie pointed to the majestic sunset. "Better than the Louvre. When the clouds are out like this. Look at all the colors filtering through them. The deep oranges. The bright reds. The clouds give a sunset life. Make it unique. If it was always a 'perfect' day, not a cloud in the sky, how boring would that be?"

"I'm impressed you knew about the Louvre," Meg teased.

"Hey…," Robbie seemed to be holding back something.

"What?"

Robbie searched for the right words when…

"Do you still make dresses?" he asked.

"Dresses…? You remember that?"

"I remember everything about that summer," Robbie smiled sweetly. "You're not easy to forget."

"Not in a long time."

"You had good designs."

"Oh, yeah, because you had such an eye for fashion," Meg teased.

Robbie shrugged. "I knew it made you happy."

"So what did you want to tell me?"

Robbie's eyes retreated from hers.

"What? Tell me."

Robbie sobered. "Why didn't you tell me about the baby?"

"Your mother just died. You had so much you were

dealing with. You said you were done with me," Meg threw it back in his face. "Remember?"

"I had a right to know. I could've helped you."

"No you couldn't've," Meg said. "We were too young. No one's ready to be a parent at sixteen."

"I raised my brothers since I was fourteen."

"Well I wasn't ready."

"Neither was I, but I did it."

"So give yourself a medal."

"How could you not want to find out if the baby was okay?"

"Because I didn't. I didn't want to get attached, okay!" Meg shouted. "I wanted to forget it ever happened."

Meg couldn't believe her own words. The self-revelation stunned her. All those years she blamed Mo for denying her pregnancy ever happened, and in truth, she was mad at herself for wanting to forget.

"I know, I'm a horrible person. That's what you want to hear me say, isn't it. This is a mistake," Meg dismissed their budding relationship, storming out to the far bow and leaving Robbie to man the wheel. "Don't follow me!" she warned. "Just get me to the dock," then she paused. "You have no idea what I went through. No idea."

The last two miles inland were filled with only the sound of the engine, the bow's breaking waters, and their thoughts.

Before Robbie moored, Meg jumped off and refused to look back. Robbie said nothing. He did not stop her. He went on as if she never boarded.

CHAPTER 15

THE DOOR COUNTIAN

Wisconsin's Largest Twice-Weekly Newspaper

Featured Columnist...
Seneca Parks

Now Hiring Still

THE POST OFFICE AT WHITEFISH CREEK has closed its doors for lack of anyone interested in serving as postmaster. Mrs. Martha Hale reports that the bother and trouble is infinitely greater than the compensation, which amounts to $215.00 a month. Anyone interested in the position, please contact our township's chairman Rufus E. Philpot.

Chairman Philpot would like to emphasize that no one has ever died as postmaster. Postmaster duties only include sorting mail and selling stamps, and are in no way, shape, or form related to the mail carrier vacancy which has been open for hire the past 17 years.

Our readers will recall that the five previous brave souls to deliver Whitefish Creek's mail all met untimely deaths: in '92, J. Milton Moon was mistaken for a deer and accidentally shot dead; in '78, Peder Skasgaard fell through the ice and drown; in '66, Orville Orsted was killed by a mail-order rattlesnake that escaped its packaging; in '49, Peder Ingwald was struck by lightning whilst loading mail inside his open barn; and the original mail carrier, Gustav Hoekendorff, was caught in the blizzard of 1927 during his route and froze to death.

Anyone interested in applying for the mail carrier vacancy, please contact Chairman Philpot directly—in addition to a good life insurance agent. Ha, ha.

In the mean time, Whitefish Creek residents can pick up their mail at Egg Harbor until a new postmaster is found.

In other news, Emmie Elefsson reports the Whitefish Creek Mercantile will be closed the next few days on account of being ransacked last night by a mad possum. Police are still puzzled why the unruly animal had a G inked on its back. Ms. Elefsson apologizes to her customers for any inconvenience.

CHAPTER 16

CHOCOLATE OIRISH TATERS

Birth makes neither sisters nor brothers,
but siblings with mutual parents;
true sisterhood and brotherhood is a condition
people must work at.

—Irish saying

MO SQUEALED WITH DELIGHT the moment Caitlyn's lights hit the shop's front window. Even before Meg's oldest sister announced plans to visit, Mo had a premonition of their arrival the moment a chair in the shop fell backwards one morning. "'Tis a sign," she insisted, swearing a fallen chair foretold a special visitor.

Mo's smiling Irish face rushed to the silver Honda Odyssey like a child ready to tear into Christmas presents. The instant its side door popped open, she jumped into the crumb-filled car, past the McDonald's wrappers, and swept her two granddaughters into her loving arms. Caitlyn's tired eyes glanced back from the driver's seat to enjoy Mo's outpouring of affection.

"Oh, let me look at you," Mo put her hands on each of her beautiful dark-haired, fair-skinned granddaughters' cheeks: Megan, 5, determined and serious; and Mary, 4, spunky, cheerful, and the spitting image of her aunt Meg. Then scrutinized the dark circles under Caitlyn's eyes.

"You have a face like the back of a bus."

"I just listened to twenty-two hours of Disney Princess DVDs," Caitlyn popped open her door.

Meg smothered her two little nieces with hugs and kisses, then exchanged cordial greetings with her big sister Caitlyn.

"Help your sister unpack," Mo instructed Meg, as she led her two granddaughters inside for homemade Irish ice cream.

The last time Meg and Caitlyn felt close was living together in a one-bedroom apartment after Meg dropped out of her senior year in high school. Meg's *magna cum laude* sister returned from Notre Dame to start a Ph.D. in genetics at Washington University in St. Louis and invited a self-destructive Meg to move in before Mo strangled her. The two fell right back into their childhood pleasures of swapping back scratches, laughing, gossiping, and indulging in late night gab sessions over their favorite childhood breakfast dish of Irish potato pancakes and syrup (Chocolate Oirish Taters), where conversation eventually turned to analyzing their crazy Irish mother. On those nights, as in childhood, the sisters fell asleep with their arms entwined like the cable knit of an Aran sweater. And true to form, Meg flourished under Caitlyn's wing. She eventually enrolled in a GED program, while they lived off Ramen noodles and spent Friday night happy hours hustling beers with their pool shark friend, Nick Bommarito, a Boston-bred medical student who Meg suspected had a deep crush on Caitlyn. They certainly enjoyed each other's company, but as Meg discovered, Caitlyn's heart lied elsewhere.

On days her older sister returned from the lab, she glowed. Caitlyn's supervisor was a distinguished geneticist who Caitlyn referred to only as "K.C.O." From what little details she revealed, he was married, had two very young children, was brilliant, a total unmade bed, funny, a complete goof, over fifteen years her senior, and someone Caitlyn never spoke of without grinning. He incited the best in her. Challenged her intellectually. You'd catch her saying "KCO thinks [this]," or "KCO did [that]," or "KCO made me laugh so hard," or "We [this]," "We [that]." As Caitlyn spent more and more late nights at the lab, Meg heard a lot of fond "we." Then one late spring evening, Caitlyn returned without the usual glow. In the days and weeks that followed, she withdrew from the world and Meg's efforts to reach out were met by a brave smile of "I'm fine," as Caitlyn buried her pain in her studies. Not long after, Meg's heartbroken sister abruptly announced plans to accept a two-year genetics fellowship in Germany. And in typical Caitlyn humility, omitted the fact she'd be working under a Nobel-laureate.

Meg was still processing all this when a broken Caitlyn presented her with a completed application to Notre Dame.

Meg's entire family grew up dyed-in-the-wool Domers under their alumnus father, with Football Saturdays qualifying as holy days of obligation to worship around the

TV and cheer for the Fighting Irish. But after her father's death, Meg detached from all things Notre Dame. Even now, it still unearthed the pain of his absence.

"I talked to a friend in admissions," Caitlyn said. "Told them about what you've gone through the past few years. They said with your high ACT scores you had a chance. Here, I filled it out. All you need to do is sign and mail it."

Meg felt so betrayed.

Caitlyn abandoned her like everyone Meg ever loved: her father, her mother when she revealed she was pregnant, Robbie, and now her only sister.

Meg threw the application into a nearby trash bin. "I would never go there!" Leaving Caitlyn a hollow shell as she stormed down the steps and into the neighborhood.

After a few blocks, Meg broke down and cried.

The application to their late father's alma mater was Caitlyn's way of looking after her. Meg knew that. Domers genuinely loved and watched over one another, like they were all part of something greater, and Caitlyn hoped that special camaraderie would care for her beloved little sister while she retreated to Germany to repair her own broken self. Meg just wanted to hurt her for leaving. She cursed Caitlyn for letting her believe she could lower her guard and depend on her.

When Meg collected her things in the apartment the day after Caitlyn's abrupt departure, a knock at the door revealed a middle-aged, disheveled man looking nervous and distraught. Meg recognized him instantly as KCO.

"Is Caitlyn here?" he clung to a shred of hope.

"No," Meg said regretfully, and watched his eyes mirror

the break of his heart.

Meg saw that Caitlyn never bid him goodbye, and probably never divulged her abrupt plans to leave. Meg never knew if Caitlyn and KCO consummated their relationship, but knowing Caitlyn, she broke it off before they committed such a "morter" (what their mother called a "mortal sin"). It wasn't in Caitlyn's nature to breakup a family no matter how much she loved him, and by the shattered look in KCO's eyes that echoed in her sister's, Meg doubted Caitlyn would ever be the same. Caitlyn gave too much of herself, let herself root too deeply, and Meg vowed never to make the same mistake.

The last decade, the sisters grew further apart as they headed down opposite roads: Caitlyn traded in her successful bio-research career for the perfect stay-at-home-mom, country club lifestyle of McMansions, McDonald's, and kids' McSoccer, raising two perfect daughters in Boston with her perfect doctor husband, while Meg partied in the Hollywood fast lane, hopping from temp job to temp job, relationship to relationship. Neither understood the other's lifestyle. Meg could no longer confide in Caitlyn without her sister's heavy judgment. And Meg felt inferior in the face of Caitlyn's "perfect" world that included a fabulous gaggle of bunco BFFs who now replaced Meg as confidant and friend.

The two of them said little as they loaded up like pack mules and headed towards the shop, when the sight of Mo's old Cadillac stopped Caitlyn in her tracks.

It sat parked at the entrance to Main Street, painted like a big tri-striped orange-white-and-green Irish flag with wheels. Mo strapped the shop's wooden *All Things Irish sign* across the car's backside and stuck an Irish flag off its front grill (Mo's answer to the City Council blocking her Irish shop with trees).

Caitlyn turned back to Meg in shock. "Mo's hit a whole new level of crazy, hasn't she?"

"And now she's alone with your daughters."

The two laughed. One thing they still shared was their mother's ridiculousness.

The next afternoon, Mo left Caitlyn and Meg to tend shop, while she took the girls to Wilson's old-fashioned ice cream parlor.

The moment Mo and the girls departed for their outing, Caitlyn explored the shop with greater detail.

"I still can't believe Mo did this," Caitlyn meandered through the shop's three moderate-sized rooms with a grand stone hearth that welcomed all visitors. Mo's pinwheel-shaped woven thrush cross of St. Brigid hung above the mantle, protecting the home from evil. And authentic goods from Ireland filled its shelves and tables, with its walls covered in Irish talismans and Notre Dame memorabilia.

Caitlyn paused at the counter, where behind it, alongside Mo's groupie-like photo of the Irish Catholic President JFK, hung a smiley picture of Meg, age 6, and Caitlyn, age 10, with arms around each other, wearing matching black skirts and white blouses at the St. Louis *oireachtas* (Irish dance championship) with Meg holding her first grand prize trophy. It was taken when the sisters were still inseparable.

"You know," Caitlyn said. "Driving here, I was thinking about that first winter I was in Germany. When you moved to L.A. and sent me that envelope filled with beach sand. No note. Just sand."

They both smiled at the memory.

"I was just being silly."

"Anytime I felt sad, all I needed to do was look at that envelope. I wouldn't have gotten through that without you."

"It was just one of my stupid pranks."

"Exactly," Caitlyn reassured her of its significance.

"Is everything okay?"

"Sure," Caitlyn answered too quickly and smiled. "Hey! Let's get drunk and make Chocolate Oirish Taters! Like we used to at our old apartment. Remember? Life was so much simpler back then," Caitlyn smiled. "You kept life simple. You always did. You were smart."

"My life is anything but simple," Meg corrected. "What's going on?"

Caitlyn pushed a smile. "Let's talk about something else. I don't want to think about it right now. I've had two years of thinking about it."

"Two years," Meg exclaimed. "What's going on?"

"Let's get drunk first," Caitlyn smiled. "I can't remember the last time I was drunk. Is there any beer?"

"There's a keg of Guinness in storage," Meg motioned to the back. "Mo got it for an Irish wedding we were planning. Then the bride got cold feet."

"Perfect," Caitlyn led the way. "So I got a joke for you. So this Englishman, Scotsman, and Irishman are sitting at a bar when three flies land in their beers…"

Ring-a-ling-ling.

They both jumped as the front door opened.

What walked into the shop was more surprising than

encountering an honest-to-goodness leprechaun. An actual customer.

CHAPTER 17

SHAMROCK SANDWICHES

When money's tight and hard to get,
and your horse is also ran;
when all you have is a heap of debt,
a pint of plain is your only man.

—*Irish saying*

A MIDDLE-AGED FISHERMAN in stained brown coveralls wandered into the shop and the sisters' jaws dropped as if he was a two-headed extraterrestrial.

"Hello," Meg almost forgot what to say. "Can I offer you some tea?"

The man held up one of Meg's gold coins. "I'd like a beer."

Meg stammered. "Oh, a, we don't…we don't actually sell beer…"

" — It says All Things Irish," the man insisted.

Meg answered his confusion with a smile that looked ready to proclaim him a lottery winner. "We sell things from Ireland — "

" — Irish Whiskey?" the man perked.

"Who needs whiskey when we have some of the world's most wonderful Aran sweaters...," Meg lifted one off the table with the charm of a seasoned salesman. "Women used to weave these back in Ireland for their husbands. And sometimes when a ship sank they knew the man's fate when his sweater washed ashore and his wife identified the pattern. These are guaranteed to outlive the wearer..."

" — Feels warm," the man begrudgingly hrumphed.

"The warmest sweater you'll ever own," Meg beamed.

"Whiskey warms me up a lot quicker!" He flashed Meg a disgusted look for luring him under false pretenses.

Ring-a-ling-ling. Three new customers walked inside. They all wore coveralls, flannel shirts, and smelled of fish.

"Forget it," the first fisherman informed the newcomers. "These coins Knudson gave us aren't worth a lick. I'm going to the Hitching Post."

Meg blocked their escape. "If you're going to drink, we have some great drinking mugs, drinking hats, drinking gloves..."

The disgruntled men pushed Meg aside when...

"Beer!" Caitlyn emerged from storage pushing a dolly with the wedding's leftover keg.

"Beer!" Meg directed their attention to the keg as Caitlyn wheeled it behind the front counter. "Who wants a beer?"

Thinking fast, Meg snatched a handful of Irish mugs from a nearby shelf: "Today only," Meg trumpeted. "Buy a twenty dollar mug, get all the free beer you can drink."

"Free?" the men roared skeptically. Then looked at one another in a moment's contemplation.

"Free," Meg confirmed.

All at once the crowd converged for $20 mugs like starving men on a food line. Meg handled the transactions while Caitlyn couldn't pour beer fast enough as more fishermen arrived. They hammed it up, drank with the crowd, hocked sweaters and hats (which Meg marketed as Irish drinking caps), sold Irish jewelry (claiming it would quell any wife's fury when the men stumbled home late that night reeking of beer), and Meg and Caitlyn laughed and carried on like they hadn't for years.

When the keg began to float, Meg called Mary Lou to run to the general store and bring reinforcements.

"Another toast! Another toast!" The crowd clamored to their two hostesses.

Meg and Caitlyn happily obliged, climbing their drunken selves atop the front counter and raising their glasses.

"Alright, alright," Meg raised her glass. "Here's to workin' like you don't need the money..." Meg started one of their late-father's favorite toasts and Caitlyn joined in with a smile. "Lovin' like you've niver been hurt...Dancin' like no-one's watchin'...SCREWIN' LIKE IT'S BEIN' FILMED...AND DRINKIN' LIKE A TRUE IRISHMAN!"

The crowd erupted with laughter and cheers, slammed their beers, and lined up for more.

"Hey!" Meg spotted Robbie pushing through the crowd and met him halfway, poking a finger into his chest. "Who said you could hand out my gold coins?"

"You left them at the Fyr Bal. I thought it might give you a few customers."

"Well I don't remember giving <u>you</u> a gold coin. You wanna drink...," Meg grabbed a fancy Waterford crystal glass and dangled it in his face. "Fifty bucks."

"Listen. I just made a delivery at the C & C. Emmie Elefsson called Baldy."

"Baldy who?"

"Our sheriff," Robbie said. "I'm guessing you don't have a liquor license."

Meg sobered. "Shit."

Then Meg heard something far worse than police sirens.

"Meg McKenna!" Mo's voice cracked like a shotgun blast.

Mo stood in the doorway with her two granddaughters reacting as if someone let loose a herd of pigs into her beautiful shop, then stared daggers at the three perpetrators.

"I expected somethin' like this from you two," Mo's terse eyes scolded Meg and Mary Lou. "But you...?" she questioned Caitlyn. "You're nothin' but a bunch of hooligans!"

Just then, an annoyed Sheriff Baldy Bridenhagen pushed his way into the unlicensed happy hour. Baldy was a few years from retirement and anything that interrupted his daily regimen of cards, cigars, and coffee was a task he wasn't getting paid enough to do, especially when antics from a bunch of FISH pulled him away from watching a Brewers' game.

"Where's the owner?" he huffed.

"I am," Mo said.

"Do you have a liquor license?" he asked, knowing the answer.

Mo spewed venom at the three hooligans. And Mary Lou made a cheerful peace offering to Mo: "Beer?"

CHAPTER 18

HOOLIGANS

When you're in jail, your good friends will always come to bail you out; your best friends will be in the cell next to you saying "damn, that was fun!"

—Anonymous Irishman

THE WORD "HOOLIGAN" first appeared in the English lexicon in the summer of 1898 after a newspaper reporting the escapades of a notoriously rowdy Irish clan of miscreants—the Houlihans—misspelled their name. When Mo threw the word at the three teetotalers, Mary Lou toasted it as one of her proudest moments. Then Baldy properly booked the four perpetrators and locked them behind bars.

Door County's jail was a turn-of-the-century brick two-story building. It consisted of a second-floor courtroom and a main-floor sheriff's office with two side-by-side jail cells separated by a concrete wall. Presently, a naked sixty-something man laid face down on the first cell's concrete floor, snoring like a drunk bear.

"Oh my god," Meg and Caitlyn burst with laughter as they sat locked in the neighboring cell.

"Jaysus, Mary and Joseph," Mo detested. "He hasn't a flitter on him!"

"Don't be such a prude," Mary Lou inhaled her contraband cigarette, extending it to Mo.

"Absolutely not!" Mo rebuffed.

"We're serving hard time, darling," Mary Lou noted, taking a puff. "You have to smoke or the rest of us inmates will think your a nancy pants and make you our bitch."

"You're daft!" Mo angrily dismissed her dramatic grandeur.

Mary Lou turned to Meg and Caitlyn. "I never had a bitch before, have you?"

"No," they both agreed with amused grins.

"I think it'd be fah-bulous," Mary Lou exhaled. "Carry our smokes, pour our wine…What about using her for sex?"

Mo shot Mary Lou the evil eye.

"Not having to deal with George begging would be a nice break," Mary Lou relished. "Although I would miss his 30 minute precursor back massages. That's usually my going rate."

"I believe massages are included in the full bitch package," Meg said.

"Marvelous," Mary Lou delighted, turning to Mo. "Then you'll be our bitch in exchange for our fahbulous protection."

Mo stared daggers: "May the curse of Mary Malone and her nine blind illegitimate children chase you so far over the hills of Damnation that the Lord Himself can't find you wid a telescope!"

The three hooligans burst out laughing.

"I don't see what's so funny about jail!" Mo raged. "Yer shenanigans turned me shop into a public house! And a *shebeen* at that."

"A she-what?" Meg laughed.

"An unlicensed drinking place," Caitlyn answered.

"We just made enough to pay off the last two months of mortgage," Meg boasted. "It's the best sales we've ever had."

"It's the only sales you've ever had," Caitlyn grinned.

"You have a gall!" Mo snapped at them. "I don't need yer shenanigans."

"You need anything you can get," Meg pushed back. "You're…," the moment the word "broke" slipped from her drunken lips, Meg knew she crossed an unforgivable line.

The two things Mo swore no respectable person ever spoke about were sex and money. Sex was just vulgar, but discussing one's financial plight in public was unpardonable.

Mo fumed. "You wanna know why you're so lost? Hoppin' from job to job and relationship to relationship. All this actin' of yers," Mo scoffed. "That's just a diversion to avoid facin' yer real problems. That's why you're so miserable. You want to find happiness, embrace yer bad luck. That's where you find out who you really are."

"Hey," Caitlyn attempted to pry apart the tension. "I never finished my joke earlier. So this Irishman, Englishman, and Scotsman are sitting at a bar when these flies…"

"Mmm huhh!" the naked man in the next cell violently cleared his throat as he stumbled to his feet.

"Oh Jaysus!" Mo averted her eyes before she glimpsed

him in full glory. Their limited adjoining view—thank God—spared them a full frontal, seeing only the side of his hands and face pressed against the neighboring bars.

"Ladies," he greeted Mo as if sauntering up to her at some pickup bar.

"You're drunk!" Mo's eyes drew on him like pistols.

The man grinned like the Cheshire Cat. "Yep. Got a hold of some bad mushrooms too. But it's the ether that's kickin' my ass."

"Ether!" Mo exclaimed. "Jaysus, Mary and Joseph. Were you tryin' to put yerself on the wrong side of the ground?"

"For the last 15 years," the man grinned. "Just not doing a good job of it." He extended his hand through the bars. "Booker Wade. Tortured writer-in-residence. I teach classes up in Ellison Bay. You should come."

"I'd rather stick needles in me eyes," Mo refused to touch his hand.

"Might help you work through all this anger," Booker smiled.

Mo's eyes flared. "I don't need any free advice, thank you very much!"

Booker apologized. "But you sure as hell strike me as someone who is in serious need of getting laid."

Mo's mouth dropped in shock as a camera flash blinded her.

"Cheese," Mary Lou's husband George snapped a picture of Mo and Naked Guy much to her horror. "This one's the Christmas card," he chuckled.

CHAPTER 19

LEGEND OF THE CLADDAGH

Let love and friendship reign supreme.

—The Claddagh's meaning

THE INSTANT GEORGE SPRUNG them from jail, Mo banished the three hooligans to the Fitzgibbons's lakeside home, making it clear she intended to enjoy the next few days doting over her two granddaughters without the likes of them.

That evening, the two inebriated sisters indulged their munchies with a festive batch of Chocolate Oirish Taters and wrapped themselves in a blanket on the Fitzgibbons' back porch with a bottle of wine—or two.

They became different people over the last decade, no longer sharing the same viewpoints or prioritizing the same things. Meg's childhood idolization of Caitlyn waned years ago. But they were still sisters. And despite clashing on most things, they never stopped caring for each other.

"There's one," Caitlyn pointed at the first shooting star.

Meg took her sister's hand and admired their family's beautiful gold Claddagh on Caitlyn's left ring finger. Six years earlier, Meg had insisted Mo pass it down to Caitlyn on her wedding day.

"One of these days we'll need to arm wrestle for it," Caitlyn smiled as she noticed Meg's interest. Caitlyn had only agreed to accept the ring on a temporary loan basis. Just until Meg became engaged and they could properly vie for it.

"You want to hear something crazy," Caitlyn raised her ring finger to the forefront. "I'm starting to think Mo's Claddagh story is real."

Meg wanted to discount such foolishness. "That's the wine talking."

For 300 years, the coveted heirloom passed to the strongest woman of each generation, along with its "curse." A curse Mo insisted turned into a blessing if you let life flow through you like a river. "Niver forget we only grow by facin' things we've niver faced before. Don't be afraid to let go of what's comfortable and embrace the difficult. That's the lesson of the Claddagh."

Mo told the story of their legendary ancestor Margaret, a pikey, who in her determination to resist life's flow placed what many deemed an inescapable curse on their lineage.

Margaret lived a transient lifestyle in the 18th century, drifting from village to village and relationship to relationship, refusing to be mired in the everyday hardships of life that she believed squelched the spirit.

As the story goes, one day a rare monsoon forced Margaret to seek refuge in the impoverished fishing village of Claddagh, where she encountered another traveler seeking shelter. He was a fisherman named Richard Joyce, who spent a life at sea, avoiding the poverty and hardships of humanity, determined to amass a small fortune to shelter him away from all the world's unpleasantries. As they anxiously waited out the storm in this godforsaken hole, the two talked and laughed for the next 24 hours, and fell deeply in love. Yet neither trusted such feelings. They had seen the hardships of life snuff out the most passionate affairs. And unbeknownst to the other, they each slipped off in the middle of the night: Margaret to a distant village, and Joyce out to sea. But no distance or time could extinguish the love they left in Claddagh.

When Margaret finally returned to the poor fishing village in search of Joyce, she heard reports that Joyce too returned looking for her, only to set sail in his quest and be captured by Algerian pirates and sold into slavery a world away. Heartbroken, Margaret prayed that all her years of avoiding hardship be delivered upon her tenfold, if her true love be returned. As a show of faith, she swore to remain in Claddagh, amidst its poverty, death, and hardship. And for ten years, she suffered with the village, helping them survive famine, war, and a horrible plague, until a strange ship appeared on its rocky shores.

Joyce returned to the destitute village, and upon seeing his beloved, dropped to his knees in jubilation. He told her about his decade in slavery to a successful Moorish goldsmith. How, over time, his hard work endeared himself to the master, and the master offered Joyce half his business, his fortune, and all the security Joyce ever sought if he married one of his beautiful daughters and became the son he always dreamed. At risk to his own life, Joyce showed the gold ring he created years before in captivity to honor the love in Claddagh he left behind. It consisted of two hands clasping a heart, with a crown resting above, signifying friendship, loyalty, and love. And the master, so taken by its beauty, released Joyce to renew the search for his beloved.

Joyce placed the Claddagh on Margaret's finger and the two committed themselves to spend the rest of their days in a simple shanty, on the shores of the impoverished village, facing all of life's hardships with a shared sense of humor and unsurpassed devotion. The ring Joyce created for Margaret grew in such popularity, it brought prominence and prosperity to the once destitute village, revealing their decade of hardship's true purpose: to save the dying village of Claddagh. And by saving others, they saved themselves.

Margaret spent the rest of her days praying that all her heirs endure unimaginable hardship in their quest for true love. For it was hardship that awakened her to the true meaning of life. And those descendants who mustered the faith, strength, and loyalty to endure this "blessing" would be rewarded with a pure love of unsurpassed happiness.

Mo McKenna's Claddagh symbolized this promise. Passed down for nearly three centuries, Mo swore it was crafted by none other than Richard Joyce himself, as evidenced by the initials engraved inside the band: "RJ".

Their late father always teased the initials read "RI", much to Mo's consternation, and impishly dismissed the chronicle of their mother's ancestral Claddagh as just more of her blarney. But Caitlyn and Meg believed. They dreamed about the promise of a great love. Yet feared the curse's foretold promise of hardship. And as children, both hoped they were strong enough to persevere.

CHAPTER 20

THE DOOR COUNTIAN

Wisconsin's Largest Twice-Weekly Newspaper

Police Report

FRIDAY NIGHT, POLICE ARRESTED a Whitefish Creek man, Booker Wade, for public intoxication and indecent exposure after Mr. Wade fired several shots over his neighbor's home, accusing them of putting a spell on his chickens to stop laying eggs.

Police responded late Friday evening to another attempted breaking-and-entering at the home of Ephraim resident, Ms. Martha Hale. The suspect remains at large.

Saturday afternoon, police apprehended four women, Mo McKenna, Meg McKenna, Caitlyn Bommarito, and Mary Lou Fitzgibbons for serving alcohol without a license inside their Whitefish Creek shop.

Police responded late Saturday evening to another breaking-and-entering at the home of Ephraim resident, Ms. Martha Hale. This time they apprehended the repeat offender in the attic. Ms. Hale failed to press charges on account it was a raccoon.

In other news, Al Johnson reported Lars the goat walking in the corral. Lars shows an obvious limp, but doctors remain hopeful of the leg's recovery. No word on whether Lars will make any rooftop appearances in the future.

CHAPTER 21

THE ORCHARD

Wine divulges truth.

—*Irish proverb*

MEG, CAITLYN, AND MARY LOU spent their exile on the beach with a stack of tabloids. They lounged in Adirondack chairs on the Fitzgibbons' back deck overlooking the bay, analyzing all the latest celeb hairstyles, fashions, diets, scandals, plastic surgeries, gossip, and weight gains, and found great solace reading about celebrities' lives more screwed up than their own.

"Good gawd!" Mary Lou held up a page. "Look at her lips. Look at this girl's fake lips. Why would you do that to yourself? It looks like she kissed an entire hive of bees. Lack of a loving father, that's what that is."

"Every time I read one these, I feel like I'm cheating on my brain," Meg delighted in her *People* magazine, then turned her attentions on Caitlyn. "So I want to hear about your moving and everything."

"What's going on?" Mary Lou raised a concerned brow.

"I got an idea," Caitlyn smiled. "Let's go to the Door County Winery. I'll tell you over a bottle."

"That's a fabulous idea," Mary Lou delighted.

"No it's not," Meg shot, feeling railroaded. "I know what you two are trying to do. He's not there."

"Then it won't matter," Caitlyn smiled.

"I'm not going," Meg said.

"After he was nice enough to pass out all those gold coins to bring in some customers...," Caitlyn pressed.

" — Which got us arrested," Meg followed.

"He tried to warn us," Caitlyn said. "Come on, it sounds like he's trying to apologize."

"Don't be such a ninny, we're going," Mary Lou marched inside to grab her keys.

Meg spent the next twenty minutes debating outfits, settling on a striking yellow sundress that didn't look like she was trying to appear striking.

Door County's cherry country boasted the perfect climate and conditions for growing its famous Montmorency cherries. Rich orchards spanned hundreds of acres with row upon row of lush cherry trees loaded with red fruit. A few roadside stands offered fresh-picked Montmorency cherries. Out in the fields, pockets of cherry pickers filled their baskets for the July harvest.

The crunch of their wheels on the gravel road alerted them to the winery's entrance, as they drove to a stop in the busy parking lot.

Up in the distance, Meg spotted the familiar, old white clapboard farmhouse where Robbie lived.

A chill prickled her body. Suddenly she felt 16 again.

She glanced around the familiar setting, taking it in like a ghost.

Then she noticed a newer one-story, red-roofed white clapboard building, with beautiful, tall, arched mutton windows. A wooden sign out front read "Wine Tasting Class at 1:00 p.m." Off its western side, overlooking the orchard, protruded a wooden deck with a dozen tables and umbrellas, filled with patrons sipping wine to an acoustic guitarist. Fifty yards back, a converted red barn housed the winemaking and storage.

The three walked passed a long sand pit with a red, handwritten sign that read "Cherry Spit Pit; Record Holder: Walter Swoboda, 7/3/2005, 17'8"."

Meg recognized the horrible penmanship as Robbie's.

They stepped inside the wine tasting building with its high, wood rafters. Several ceiling fans lazily churned the warm summer air. A crowd lined the wine bar while three hostesses offered generous pours. One swirled her glass, instructing a small group about a wine's "legs."

Meg admired the shop's quaint decorating, with its tall windows overlooking the cherry orchard. Soft light danced in all the right places, highlighting its treasure trove of merchandise: wooden wine boxes, books, fancy corkscrews, lovely picnic baskets, wine casks, cherry jams, cheeses, and other darling accessories.

A tall, beautiful blond Viking-esque warrior of a woman in her mid-30s stepped over to them.

"How are you ladies?" she greeted them with a friendly smile. "Can I interest you in our tasting?"

"That would be fabulous," Mary Lou said.

The woman set three wine glasses on the counter and poured. "I think you'll really enjoy this. This is our award-winning blackberry select. It won the gold medal at this year's International Eastern Wine Competition. It's perfect for a hot summer day like today."

Mary Lou sipped. "Fabulous."

"I love all your displays," Meg said.

"That's sweet, thanks," she grinned modestly, appreciating the compliment.

"I know Robbie didn't design them," Meg laughed at the idea.

"Do you know Robbie?" the girl's eyes honed on Meg like lasers.

"Old friends," Meg said.

"Is Robbie around?" Caitlyn asked hopefully.

"I don't think so," she said. "Are you all from around here?"

"My husband's family has had a place in Whitefish Creek for three generations," Mary Lou answered. "This is marvelous," Mary Lou wiggled her empty glass for another pour. "Thank you, darling."

"You come up every summer?" the woman asked Meg.

"Since they were in diapers," Mary Lou said.

"So how do you know Robbie?" the woman held her grin.

"He used to deliver fish," Meg downplayed their past relationship.

The woman smiled with some ease, but kept her eyes on Meg. "Sounds like Robbie delivered fish to everyone up here at one time."

"I guess he did," Meg smiled lightly.

The woman poured more, not quite lowering her radar.

"I'm sorry, I'm Anna," she grinned. "I manage the winery."

Anna, Meg's mind swam. The name Alewife Alma mentioned at dinner.

Mary Lou extended her hand. "Mary Lou, darling. This is Caitlyn and Meg—my two divine nieces."

The moment Mary Lou said Meg's name, a light bulb lit in Anna's eyes. No doubt she heard about the Fyr Bal incident and secret love child. And since she knew Robbie, probably more.

"Nice to meet you," they all responded in kind.

Anna pulled another sample bottle. "You'll really like this. This is our cherry blossom wine. It's slightly more sweet than the other..." She poured full glasses as if dispensing truth serum. "But a little more alcohol. It's one of my favorites. Especially on hot days."

The girls tasted the fruity kicker, much to their delighted palate. Meg found it a little too sweet.

"So are you up here for a week?" Anna served another friendly question.

"I am," Caitlyn offered after her sip.

"What about you?" Anna asked Meg.

"Only until I can get out of here," Meg said.

Anna smiled curiously. "Why do you say it like that?"

"I'm from L.A."

Anna beamed. "L.A. That sounds a lot more exciting than this sleepy lil' ol' place. What's keeping you here?"

"I'm helping my mom."

"With that Irish shop?" Anna seemed all too familiar for Meg's comfort.

"Yes. So you run the winery?" Meg asked, curious to ascertain Anna's relationship with Robbie.

"Robbie and I started it together," she emphasized *together*. Then she laughed. "Robbie doesn't exactly have the most sophisticated palette. He can't tell the difference between a ten-dollar bottle and a hundred-dollar one. I guess that's how he's able to eat all that God-awful lutefisk."

Under any other circumstance Meg would've laughed. It was a joke she shared. But hearing Anna say it with such familiarity unsettled her.

"So you have the whole Door talking about you and Robbie," Anna added fearlessly. "Robbie said you gave up the baby for adoption."

Anna's frankness stunned Meg like a blast of ice water to the face.

"It's hard being a mother so early," Anna said. "I had my daughter senior year in high school. The father turned out to be a complete loser. But you find a way to get through it. It made me grow up. Made me stronger. And it eventually led me here. Robbie's been a wonderful father figure to my daughter. And if business will slow down just a minute, we're hoping to set a date to get married this winter," she smiled large for Meg's benefit.

A sick squeeze pained Meg's stomach as she forced a smile: "Congratulations."

"Thanks," Anna grinned, knowing Meg felt queasy from the venom. "We're talking about getting married on Lighthouse Island."

Meg's chest tightened. The idea of Anna and Robbie marrying at such a sacred watershed in her life sickened her. She had resisted the temptation to visit Lighthouse Island since returning to the Door. Part of her wanted to preserve the memory she kept sacred these last fourteen years. Part of her feared the emotions it might uncork. Still, another part yearned to see it. Needed to see it. Hoped to experience the ghosts of her past, and maybe, just maybe, feel a remnant of innocence and magic of her first love. And the idea of Robbie marrying anyone else there felt like a betrayal of that memory.

"I always thought it'd be the perfect place for a wedding," Anna continued. "Right as the sun's going down. It's so romantic."

Meg couldn't breathe.

"Have you ever heard the story about its ghost?" Anna twinkled. "They say some nights, the ghost of the first keeper's widow stands in the tower looking for her husband to return from the Civil War — "

" – We've heard it," Meg cut her off sharply.

"I think it's so romantic. Janet," Anna called over one of the other wine girls. "Will you take over these wonderful ladies' samplings? I need to go back to the cellar," Anna turned to three of them. "It was nice meeting you all. Enjoy your visit."

Not two seconds after Anna took herself out of earshot, Mary Lou released an exasperated gasp. "Good gawd, she did everything but mark him with her urine."

Caitlyn nodded in agreement.

The sickness in Meg's stomach mixed with the growing

anger towards Robbie's failure to mention Anna.

Caitlyn attempted to divert her sister's anguish. "Hey, let me finally tell you about the Irishman and the fly…"

"I'm going out to the car," Meg abandoned her wine glass.

Gravel crunched at her feet as she stormed across the parking lot in a tempest of emotions until she reached Mary Lou's Explorer and caught her breath. Her insides squeezed into a hard knot.

Meg tried to cram her feelings into that deep place that couldn't hurt her. She attempted to walk off the pain, then as she turned back towards the winery, off in the distant barn, she spotted Robbie in jeans, unbuttoned flannel, and a cherry-stained white T-shirt, maneuvering a dolly full of cherry-filled crates, with the help of what looked like a teenage girl who resembled Anna. They were goofing around with each other, laughing like father and daughter. The teenager threw a cherry at Robbie, and he promptly retaliated with a handful from one of the crates. Then Anna walked out to them, and they both bombarded her.

Meg felt like some voyeuristic cutter as she watched this perfect little family.

Then Robbie glanced her way.

Meg's emotions polarized as he spotted her. Then Anna and the girl spied her as well.

Meg fast retreated to the shelter of the car as if a mortar shell screamed her way.

She popped open the driver side door, jumped in, slammed it, reached for the ignition, and realized Mary Lou had the keys.

A moment later Robbie appeared outside the door and Meg refused to make eye contact. "You okay?"

"I'm fine." She was the farthest thing from fine.

"Do you want to talk about it?"

Meg forced a smile and shook her head, no eye contact. "That's what you wanted to tell me on the boat the other day."

Robbie nodded regretfully. "Anna and I — "

" — Don't...," Meg's hand halted him.

"We've been on and off again — "

Meg waved it off. " — It's not a big deal."

"Right before you showed up, Anna and I committed to trying one last time. We started talking about marriage, maybe possible dates — "

"You don't need to explain. We're good. I'm leaving at the end of the month anyway."

"Riley's been a part of my life since she was seven. We raised her like she was both our daughter while we were startin' this business together..."

" — You don't need to explain..." Meg mustered her most courageous smile and looked right into his distraught blue eyes. "You look like a nice family."

"I waited for you for a long time," Robbie said sadly. "Every summer. I knew I acted bad when you left. I called you..."

Meg didn't believe it. "No you didn't."

"I left messages for like six months after you left."

"With who?"

"Your parents. They always said you were out. And when you never called back, I thought you never wanted to speak to me again."

"I was in Ireland. I never got your messages."

Robbie lowered his head into his chest. "I can't believe you show up now. Of all times. When I thought you were finally out of my head…"

" — What?" Meg grabbed his last statement.

"Nothing."

"Listen," Meg grew angry over the situation. "This whole 'you and I,' it's not real. I read somewhere once that first love memories are so strong, the compulsion to go back to them is as basic as hunger. That's all this is."

"What?"

"It said first love memories actually become a physical part of the person," Meg continued. "Sometimes impossible to get rid of. Like a basic instinct. And once I'm gone, none of this will matter. Go back to your family."

Robbie wanted to say more.

"Please go," Meg felt herself breaking. "Just go."

And reluctantly, slowly, Robbie departed.

CHAPTER 22

THE ROCKY ROAD TO DUBLIN

When God sends you down a stony path,
may He give you strong shoes.

—*Irish saying*

CAITLYN LOOKED LIKE the proverbial deer in headlights when they returned from the winery. Every muscle inside her clinched as she stepped into the Irish shop.

The happy giggles and shrieks of her girls gave way to the unmistakable velvet laughter of her husband, Nick Bommarito, their old St. Louis friend and pool shark buddy. Nick started aggressively courting Caitlyn the moment she ended her German exile to accept a Harvard fellowship in his hometown of Boston. And despite Caitlyn's initial reluctance to extend their relationship beyond "good friends," Nick's persistence paid off and they announced their wedding in Caitlyn's and Nick's typical mischievous humor:

Mrs. Moira "Mo" McKenna
Ecstatically Announces
Her Eldest Daughter,
Caitlyn Ann,
Will (Finally) Be
Married To The Boston Billiard Champ,
Nick Bommarito, M.D.
(minor in medicine)
In St. Louis, Missouri, at 5:00 P.M.
On Friday, April 23
At the Church of St. Peter's

Nick's voice sobered her.

Walking to the back room, she saw him playfully crawling on all fours like a crab, grasping at the girls with his "pinchers" as they squealed with terrified delight. Nick and the girls invented all kinds of crazy games for their amusement and Crab was their all-time favorite.

"Mommy!" Megan lit up. "Daddy's back! See! Daddy's here! He says he's coming home!"

Caitlyn smiled for the benefit of her daughters.

"Cait," Nick smiled hopefully.

"What are you doing here, Nick? You should be in San Diego."

"I missed my three girls."

Caitlyn tilted her head skeptically. "You had a chance to see us two weeks ago and missed your plane."

"I need to be closer to home," he approached. "I've already made arrangements at that place in Springfield — "

Caitlyn's sharp eyes deterred Nick from stepping closer. "We can talk about this later."

"I need to be closer to home — "

" — We'll talk later," Caitlyn kept a measured tone, noticing her 5-year-old daughter tuned in.

"Why don't you want daddy home?" Megan accused Caitlyn.

Caitlyn gazed empathetically at her daughter whose eyes mirrored the confusion on her face. "Oh, I do sweetheart. It's not that."

"Girls," Mo tried to redirect her granddaughters' attention. "Who wants to go to their Auntie Lou's and make double fudge brownie shakes?"

"Yeay!" Mary cheered.

"Is daddy coming?" Megan demanded.

"In a wee bit," Mo informed her granddaughter. "Let's let him and yer mum talk."

"He's coming right?" Megan said, refusing to move.

"Of course, luv," Mo said. "They just need to have a little chinwag, that's all. They'll be along shortly. Come on now."

Megan stared at her mother ruefully. "Why are you being so mean to daddy?"

"Now Meg-pie," Nick smiled. "I'll be right behind you. Why don't you make one of those brownie shakes for me and I'll see you in a few minutes."

"With sprinkles, daddy?" Mary beamed.

"Yes, Mary-Mary-Quite-Contrary!" Nick delighted. "And don't forget the whipped cream."

Mary's smile widened at the thought of drinking shakes

with her daddy. Megan was reluctant to take her suspect eyes off Caitlyn, until Mo's authoritative tone insisted she step in line and follow them out the door.

Later that night, after Caitlyn put the girls to sleep in one of the Fitzgibbons' bedrooms, Meg, Mo, Caitlyn and Mary Lou powwowed on the back deck to hear her confession.

"He lost his medical license a year ago," Caitlyn began. "They revoked it. Permanently."

"What?!" Mo exclaimed. "Why?"

"He was writing illegal scripts. To fake patients. He was using some, selling others. Then he started writing scripts with his partners' names and forging their signatures. They found out and turned him in."

"Why would he do that?" Mo failed to comprehend.

"He's an addict."

"I can't believe it," Meg said.

"He was hiding money and using it for drugs. He sold illegal scripts to support his habit...used some of the money for this lavish lifestyle he wanted to live."

"Jaysus, Mary and Joseph," Mo gasped.

"The IRS caught him for tax evasion. It cost us everything we ever saved to get him off. We had to sell the house…"

"Oh my gosh," Meg said, as guilt twisted the pit of her stomach for ever wishing ill on her sister's perfect world. "I'm so sorry."

"We have nothing now. Nothing. We're in so much debt. Lawyers' fees. Back taxes. I had to go back to work. We lost all our medical coverage. We've been paying everything out-of-pocket for over a year. My health insurance through Harvard doesn't officially kick in until next month. Now my wages are being garnished. We had to borrow money from his parents to put him in this hardcore drug boot camp in San Diego. It was one of the stipulations of his probation. He's been out there two months. No contact with the outside world. I told the girls he was out there for work."

Mo placed a consoling hand on Caitlyn's, and Caitlyn glanced up appreciatively.

"Two weeks ago," Caitlyn choked. "He got his first weekend leave. He was supposed to fly back for a few days. He never made his plane. He went to an ATM and withdrew the little savings we had left, then disappeared. We didn't know where he was for three days. The police found him in Tijuana. Now he's back in rehab. Or at least was. I worry about the girls. They're such good kids. They were heartbroken when he didn't show."

They all felt horrible, but wanted to be strong for Caitlyn.

"You know what's the funny thing about this," Caitlyn smiled mournfully. "Nick had to have all the gourmet appliances. A hundred thousand dollar kitchen renovation. Marble bathrooms. Expensive furniture. The perfect cars. The perfect clothes. I even let myself get caught up in it. It seemed so important. Just a bunch of stupid symbols. That's all they ever were. And for what? All the pressure he put on himself to achieve the great 'American dream.' That's what did it to him. And you know what's the ironic tragedy of it all," Caitlyn smiled bitterly. "You don't realize that 'dream' was never your own until it's too late."

"Well maybe this is just the thing you needed to right the ship," Mo said. "All Irish luck is a blessin' — "

Meg groaned at her mother's tired maxim.

"Well it's true!" Mo insisted.

But Meg didn't care. She turned, enraged, and tearful to Caitlyn. "You're an asshole!"

Caitlyn drew back in shock, then bowed her head admittedly. "I know I haven't been the best sister the last few years — "

" — you've been an asshole!"

"I was so frustrated with my own life, feeling so trapped, and here you are, no ties, I was jealous. And I took it out on you. I'm sorry. I'm really sorry."

"Did you know every time we talked I'd hang up feeling like shit because of all your judgment and snide comments?"

"I'm sorry."

"You were always the one I counted on," Meg looked sad. "I wished this upon you."

"What?" Caitlyn startled.

"I wished for something to knock you off your perfect little pedestal."

For the first time in Meg's life, Caitlyn glared at her with contempt. "You self-absorbed little snot. Now who's the hypocrite? You want to talk 'perfect.' You're the one who's created this perfect little world where you can't get hurt. No long-term job, no long-term relationship, no worries, no attachments. Cut ties if things get too rocky or complicated. That's what you did to me. Things got a little too hairy so you cut me out of your life. And don't think I didn't feel that, too."

An upset Caitlyn stood to leave.

"You're going back to him, aren't you," Meg stated disapprovingly.

"It's not about me anymore. It's about my family. That's the commitment I made. Something you have no concept of."

The next afternoon, Caitlyn headed for Boston with Nick and the two girls.

For the first time, Meg and Caitlyn parted without saying "I love you."

CHAPTER 23

OIRISHNESS

It takes time to build castles.

—*Irish saying*

UNLIKE RATIONAL CONSUMERS who entered a store with a desire to purchase something specific—Irish customers shopped like sugar-deprived ADHD kindergartners on a candy binge. In one splurge, they'd buy a beautiful Claddagh necklace, some Waterford crystal, an Aran sweater, a Madonna statuette, Tayto Crisps, Barry's Irish Tea, an Ireland rugby jersey, and a little book of Irish toasts. There was no rhyme or reason what they consumed, as long as it bore the shape or emblem of a shamrock, leprechaun, Claddagh, an orange-white-and-green tri-striped flag, or sported the name "Ireland" or "Irish." Mary Lou swore if you took a pile of dog shit, shaped it into a four-leaf clover, by week's end, you'd sell a dozen.

Irish shoppers came in varying degrees of Irishness, too. You had your true *Irish* (born and raised in Ireland). And your *Irish Americans* (offspring whose parents hailed from

Ireland). But the kind who frequented the upper-peninsula were more the wannabe Irish: *O'mericans* (offspring with traceable Irish-American lineage); *McIrish* or *O'Irish* (Americans with merely Irish last names); and *e pluribus Irish* (Notre Dame grads who considered themselves Irish by degree).

Meg, Mo, and Mary Lou once listened to two older O'merican women posturing over who visited Ireland more times, who boasted more Irish relatives, who flew the flag higher, who sent more children to Notre Dame, who kissed the Blarney Stone more...

"You know the locals pee on it," Meg stopped them cold. "Oh, yeah, it's a big pastime over there. After a night at the pub, they break into the castle and use it as a urinal. Then spend the next day laughing at all the busloads of tourists that pull into town to kiss it."

Meg smiled at their aghast faces, watching their lips sour. As it turned out, neither woman was even Irish. They married into McIrish families—although one insisted her great-great-great-great grandmother was a quarter Irish.

A smattering of guests wandered off the street inquiring if they sold Scandinavian stuff, Italian gifts, German, English, or knew of any shops that did.

"Gawddamn stupid people," Mary Lou cursed. "I swear, there are so many more stupid people in the world today. Back when we were growing up, stupid kids either got electrocuted or run over by cars. Now there's too many laws protecting them. You see the warning label they have on lawnmowers, big capitol letters: 'Do not operate in water.' You know that right there saved about 50 retards!"

They even heard the proverbial tourist questions like "So what do you folks do around here during the winter?"

"Dress warmer," Mary Lou retorted.

Mo greeted them all with equal Irish hospitality: "Come in and take the weight off;" "You'll have a spot of tea?;" "Are you fer raisin bread?" And those angry summerers who stormed in to give an earful about tarnishing the village's Scandinavian persona, often left befuddled by Mo's charm, enjoying a delicious slice of raisin bread they hoped to hate.

"If you like it, mail me a check," Mo often extended guests the courtesy of paying for merchandise later. "If not, bring it back."

This practice frustrated Meg to no end, making it difficult to keep accurate books or pay monthly bills.

"Are we practicing reverse layaway now?" Meg chided Mo.

One sickly septuagenarian absentmindedly left her purse back home in Milwaukee, so Mo insisted she take the nine Aran Sweaters she picked out for her grandchildren and just mail a check. Mo even gave her the last $20 from the till to use for gas money and never bothered obtaining the woman's contact information.

"She's a good Catholic," Mo reassured Meg, after the woman walked away with over $1,200 in merchandise.

The week after Caitlyn departed, an awful stench permeated the shop, repelling customers.

"It smells like a gawddamn cow pasture!" Mary Lou winced, the hot temperatures preventing them from closing the windows in their non-air conditioned shop.

The mounting smell led them to the woods behind the

shop where thick, thorny brush hindered entry. Ten yards back, an enormous minefield of big animal droppings baked under the hot mid-July sun.

"Something doesn't smell right about this," Mary Lou surmised. "And it's not the shit. This isn't another one of your boyfriend's pranks?" Mary Lou confronted Meg.

"It's not him," Meg said with absolute certainty. "And he's not my boyfriend. We haven't spoken in weeks."

The first half of July, Meg watched Robbie drive his truck down Whitefish Creek to make his daily deliveries, and every time, Meg's heart quickened, secretly hoping he'd stop.

Meg thought about riding her bike up to the fishermen's dock on a few occasions but convinced herself that nothing good could come of it.

Robbie, Anna, and Riley were a family. Like Caitlyn with KCO, Meg cared too much for Robbie to turn his moral compass anywhere but north.

Robbie remained the barometer for every guy she dated. She thought about him over the years. Wondered how he was doing. And now that she knew, it felt like a deep emotional gash no tourniquet could fix.

Like her sister with KCO, she retreated. For two weeks, she wandered around the shop like a depressed spirit, no appetite, living in neither this world nor the hereafter, with no Robbie or Caitlyn in her life.

"Good gawd," Mary Lou burst. "It's been two weeks. If you don't snap out of this, I'll put you out of your misery like a gawddamn lame horse."

Meg stood behind the counter, brooding over Caitlyn's accusation of not committing to anything, when the *jing-a-*

ling-ling of the front door opened with the faint linger of the backyard manure pile they buried with shovels. They almost failed to recognize Booker Wade with clothes—snakeskin boots, jeans, and leather biker's jacket—until they heard his unmistakable cackle.

"Don't you have a home to go to?" Mo confronted him at the door.

"Don't get your pantyhose all in a tussle. I'm heading to North Dakota. I meet up with some old buddies every year at Sturgis. One of 'em's a big Mic. Thought I'd bring him something. You got any *Kiss Me I'm Irish* T-shirts…? Thought it might help him with the ladies."

Mo spat venom. "I'd rather have me eyes scrambled with a red hot poker than sell such tripe."

Booker grinned, undaunted. "Mind if I look around?" Booker smiled cordially, and against Mo's better judgment, she allowed him passage. Hat Guy stared him down from the nearby hat shelf as Booker cased the place, stopping to admire a thick, black wooden cane of some sort. "Looks like you can bash someone pretty good with this," Booker swung it and Hat Guy jumped.

"'Tis a shillelagh," Mo kept a tight eye on him.

"I like it," he grinned, then noticed Hat Guy staring daggers. "Nice hat."

Hat Guy looked away.

"That's fragile," Mo warned Booker as he manhandled a crystal bowl.

Booker set it down. "Nice place. You should really think about getting some of those *Kiss Me I'm Irish* T-shirts…"

" — Get out!" Mo snapped.

"You wouldn't carry any shamrock-printed bongs?"

Mo was appalled and cursed him. "May you die roarin' like Doran's arse! Go!"

Booker grinned, exiting to the *jing-a-ling-ling* of Mo's pixy-like bell that jingled each time a customer opened the door.

"Gobshite!" she spat under her breath.

Meg walked over. "He just shoplifted that shillelagh."

"What?!"

Mo and Meg darted out front to watch Booker roar off on his Harley with the tip of the shillelagh protruding from the motorcycle's rear pack.

"He's as crooked as a ram's horn," Mo cursed.

"At least he wore clothes this time," Meg noted.

"Put silk on a pig, 'tis still a pig."

The next day, a hollow Meg announced her departure. "My manager called. There's an audition she thinks I'd be perfect for. I need to be back in L.A. by next week, so I'm heading out tomorrow. She already bought me a ticket. I can bunk with her for a little while."

Meg needed to sever all ties with Robbie if she hoped to move on with life, and made Mo promise not to divulge her whereabouts should Robbie ask.

Before she boarded a plane for L.A., she organized Mo's notebook of financial scribbles into a coherent ledger. Meg calculated all monthly cost, itemized assets and liabilities, created a professional balance sheet and cash flow statement, dictated minimum profit margins, and concluded if sales continued at the current pace until Labor Day, the shop would not generate enough cash to survive the winter.

CHAPTER 24

THE IRISH ROVER

We had sailed seven years when the measles broke out, and the ship lost its way in a fog.

And that whale of the crew was reduced down to two, just meself and the captain's old dog.

Then the ship struck a rock, oh Lord what a shock, the bulkhead was turned right over.

Turned nine times around, and the poor dog was drowned, I'm the last of the Irish Rover.

—*The Irish Rover lyrics*

LIFE SINCE RETURNING to the Hollywood scene seemed empty. Even when she landed her first TV acting gig in five years, her heart remained empty. Nothing about this glam lifestyle filled Meg with any real sustenance. In her two months since the Door, none of the quick fixes, the parties, the shopping sprees, the glitz and glamour fed her soul. Conversations Meg once thought so fabulous now felt like bad junk food that left your body aching for nutrition. Meg couldn't believe all this mattered to her for the last decade. And for what?

When she looked in the mirror, her mother was right. She wasn't acting to act. It offered an excuse to avoid facing her own demons.

It was a far cry from her mother's lifestyle of welcoming both the good and bad in life.

Meg found herself watching sunsets. And just as Robbie noted, the blemish of clouds on an otherwise "perfect" day elevated each sunset to a unique masterpiece of colors and strokes, inspiring anyone who slowed long enough to partake.

Meg heard Robbie visited the shop a few weeks after she departed. And true to Mo's word, she declined to divulge Meg's whereabouts.

As July rolled into August, and August into September, Mo provided updates on Caitlyn. They hired an ex-nurse named Irene to watch the girls during the week, which Meg knew crushed her big sister. Megan started lashing out at Caitlyn for working. "Irene's a better mommy than you," a resentful Megan struck at Caitlyn's Achilles heel. "At least she's around to play with us."

Mo said Irene was a plain woman in her mid-thirties, a former nurse of Nick's, who apparently suffered a nervous breakdown a year earlier, which Nick insisted was merely burnout from a high-stress ER position. She agreed to work for half the price of anyone equally qualified. Yet Mo reported that something about Irene made Caitlyn uneasy. Even though she played well with the girls, it bothered Caitlyn that Irene turned quiet whenever Caitlyn stepped into the room. She never acted that way around Nick, which made Caitlyn uncomfortable. But with little money, Caitlyn had no alternative.

"She asked about you too," Mo informed Meg about Caitlyn. "You need to call each other and talk."

The last week of September, Meg decided to visit an Irish pub—The Mad Fiddler—a popular destination for visiting Irishmen that offered a nice cure for Irish homesickness. Her TV gig had ended and she was back to her transient life. She had rented a spare bedroom from an old friend who was away on a 6-month production shoot. As she nursed a beer at the bar, listening to the rugby crowd shout at the TV and a cute couple giggling in the corner, Meg contemplated calling Caitlyn. She wanted to know how long it took her to recover from KCO. The same heartache Meg suffered now. Then her cell phone buzzed. It was her mother.

Meg watched it buzz three times before she decided to answer. Mo sounded full of tears. And Meg braced for something terrible.

"It's Caitlyn," Mo choked. And the unsettling words that followed brought the sky crashing upon Meg's world.

CHAPTER 25

THE FIGHTING IRISH

A family of Irish birth will argue and fight, but let
a shout come from without, and see them all unite.

—*Irish saying*

"WE'LL FIGHT THIS," Mo trumpeted. "Fight it like Irishmen."

Mo was fiercely proud of her culture's fighting Irish reputation. A nickname later given to New York City's tenacious Civil War Brigade of gritty Irish immigrants, whose chaplain, William Corby, rallied them at the Battle of Gettysburg and eventually became the third president of a little known college in Indiana called Notre Dame. East Coasters referenced the school as that "Fighting Irishman's University." And years later, legend held that during a Notre Dame-Michigan football game, as a beaten down Notre Dame returned to their locker room at half, one Irish-American player yelled at a group of teammates "What's the matter with you guys? You're all Irish and you're not fighting worth a lick!" Then Notre Dame retook the field to defeat

Michigan, prompting one Chicago reporter who overheard the remark (and knew Corby's legacy) to tout the game as a victory for the "Fighting Irish," forever endearing the name into pop culture lexicon.

Caitlyn was one of the Fighting Irish, not only in degree, but in blood and spirit. She fought for everything she earned. She attributed her grades to ten percent brains and ninety percent hard work. Her Irish dancing accomplishments to training harder than her far more talented competitors. Her lab success to tenacity. If anyone could beat cancer, it was Caitlyn.

When Meg arrived at Logan International Airport in Boston, she found her mother waiting at the gate, sitting in a row of chairs, her lips moving silently as she said the rosary.

Meg walked over and smiled softly, waiting for Mo to finish the last few prayer beads.

"The car's parked outside," Mo stood. No hug. No *hello*. No *how was yer flight*. She was a woman possessed. "Yer sister's already in surgery. We need to get there," Mo headed straight to the parking lot where the Irish mobile sat.

Thirty minutes later they arrived at the hospital.

They found Nick sitting nervously on the couch in the stark waiting room, with his mother and sister, both short, dark-skinned Italians.

The Bommaritos greeted them with sincere smiles and big Italian hugs, and Nick's eyes looked worried.

"How is she?" Mo asked, gripping his wrists.

"She's been in almost four hours," Nick said. "The doctor said if it's a short surgery that meant there was nothing they could do."

"Four hours is good then," Mo said, clutching to hope.

"Very," Nick said. "Her other results came in last night. They looked a lot more encouraging than the ones before. A lot more."

After an hour of watching each tick of the clock and listening to the clack of Mo's rosary beads, the adrenalin that carried Meg through the past 24 hours dissipated and she headed to the cafeteria to retrieve stiff coffee and sandwiches for everyone.

"Let me help you," Nick announced. "It's on me."

Nick seemed deep in thought as they walked down the sterile corridor to the elevator, when he angrily blurted: "Her doctor did this to her. Her primary care. He misdiagnosed her a year ago," he glared with a vengeful determination that made Meg uncomfortable. "Don't you or Mo worry. I'm going to sue him for everything he's got."

His words took Meg aback. She couldn't believe he broached this with Caitlyn still in surgery. Her sister would never entertain such things. Never.

When the elevator doors opened, Nick excused himself for a smoke.

"Grab me a tuna, will ya," Nick grinned. "I'll be there in a minute to help."

Meg waited with a full tray of food in the cafeteria for over ten minutes and Nick never returned. She finally grew sick of waiting, paid, and returned to the eighth-floor waiting room where she found Nick sitting on the couch.

"Here, let me help you," he jumped to the tray, passing out the drinks to everyone.

"Where'd you go?" Meg asked. "I thought you were

coming back."

"I did. I didn't see you," Nick smiled.

"I was there," Meg found his excuse lacking.

Nick shrugged. His eyes looked mellow. He smelled of peppermint. And Meg suspected Nick smoked something other than cigarettes.

Another hour passed before Caitlyn's middle-aged surgeon, Dr. Bill Madison, appeared in full scrubs, with his mask pulled down around his neck.

Everyone jumped up searching for any hint of optimism in his perfunctory expression.

"We're still in surgery," he noted, everyone hanging on each word. "I just wanted to give you an update. I think we got everything we could see, but it was worse than we anticipated."

Everyone's heart stopped.

"It was on the underside of her stomach, which is why the earlier test results were erratic. We had to remove her entire stomach..."

They all gasped.

"I took out a good part of her esophagus. As much as I safely could. We took out the spleen. A good part of her intestine. We'll know a little more in a few days when we get the tests back. We also had to give her a colostomy."

Mo squeezed Meg's hand so fiercely it cut circulation.

"On most people I would've just closed them up," the surgeon said. "Her quality of life won't be good the next six months. She'll need to undergo chemo and radiation. The oncologist can tell you more about that. But Caitlyn's young. She's strong. Before we put her under, she made me promise to give her a fighting chance. That's what I did. Like I said, I think I got it all. Everything I could see. We'll wait and see what the test results show. It'll be another good hour before she's in the ICU."

The surgeon offered a faint smile of hope.

"What are her chances?" Nick asked.

The surgeon looked him straight in the eye. "It's one of the most aggressive cancers."

"What are her chances?" Meg demanded.

"Statistically, less than six percent survival rate past the first year."

Meg felt her knees buckle.

Nick shrunk.

"She's a fighter," Mo insisted, trying to elicit better odds.

"Good," Dr. Madison said empathetically. "That will serve her well."

"She can live without a stomach?" Meg asked an almost trivial point under the circumstances.

"She won't be able to eat as much, but yes. She can. She'll need to eat more little meals a day once she's off the G-tube. That won't be for another month."

Dr. Madison excused himself back to the operating room, then stopped, and his perfunctory demeanor softened.

"They've studied people who survive this," Dr. Madison said. "Are you religious?"

"Yes," Mo said resolutely.

"Look. Most of my colleagues would disagree. But I've seen miracles in my thirty-two years of medicine. Things that conventional science can't explain. I've seen a handful of people who made it through the first year and lived a long life without recurrence. Most all these people had tight families. Just about all of them prayed. I really believe there's something to that. It's no guarantee, but I think it increases your odds." Then he offered a warm, self-deprecating grin. "As much as we surgeons like to believe we're God, our powers have limits. His don't."

The surgeon offered a hopeful smile before leaving everyone to process the desperate news.

Meg suddenly felt both her hands gripped by Mo. "Caitlyn will fight this," Mo stared intently at her. "We'll all fight this."

"We will," Meg looked into her eyes and said what they both needed to believe in their hearts.

"Our darling girl," Mo smothered Meg with an embrace. Both clung to each other for dear life in the face of this tornado. And unlike fourteen years earlier, when Meg boarded the plane to Ireland, neither let go prematurely.

When they finally saw Caitlyn lying on a gurney in the ICU, she looked a pale shell of the person who visited them over the summer. Nick thought it best she hear the prognosis from Mo and Meg, then excused himself for a smoke before they entered the ICU, returning ten minutes later smelling of peppermint.

Mo held tight to Caitlyn's hand as she gazed upon her with a loving smile.

Meg and Nick stood bedside, both smiling compassionately.

Caitlyn closed her heavy eyes for a moment to swallow, then reopened with a brave sense of purpose. "Did it metastasize?"

Mo maintained her loving grin and nodded. "They removed yer stomach," Mo said, incrementally continuing as if wading into frigid water. "They also found some in yer colon."

Caitlyn shut her eyes with a sad expression of hopelessness.

Nick interjected. "The good news is they think they got it all."

Nick's words fell on deaf ears.

Even in such a groggy state, Caitlyn knew, from a purely scientific standpoint, stomach cancer that metastasized was a death sentence.

She dedicated a career to finding a cure for cancer through genetic research, and now the irony of her fate was not lost.

Caitlyn squeezed her eyes shut, fighting back tears.

Her primary care's diagnosis of a benign cyst over a year ago was completely wrong. Had she not been in the thick of everything with Nick, right when they lost their health insurance, she would've pursued it more aggressively and discovered it was a malignant tumor that needed immediate surgery. And the doctors most likely would've removed it before it metastasized.

Mo squeezed Caitlyn's left hand tight. "We'll call upon the Blessed Virgin. She can work miracles. She'll see us through this."

Caitlyn appreciated their words, but the reality stifled her. She knew her odds. And the thought of her two young girls without a mom made her turn her heavy head into the hospital pillow to let drain the rush of tears.

She probably had less than six months to live.

CHAPTER 26

AN IRISH BLESSING

May the road rise to meet you,
may the wind be always at your back,
may the sun shine warm upon your face,
may the rains fall soft upon your fields,
and until we meet again,
may God hold you in the palm of His hand.

—Irish blessing

MARY LOU HELD VIGIL the day of Caitlyn's surgery with over a hundred old friends back in their St. Louis parish church of St. Peter's. The next morning, she flew to Boston to levitate the atmosphere with her frank sense of humor and no-nonsense New England attitude.

"No stomach. That's fabulous. You'll never gain weight again."

She spent the next few days praying over Caitlyn with Mo, calling upon the Holy Mother to bless over their dear girl, saying rosaries, taking the graveyard watch over Caitlyn so Mo and Meg could rest, and as abruptly as she arrived, flew back to St. Louis the day after Caitlyn's release because "I'd only get in the way, darling."

Caitlyn returned home in a lot of pain. She was on morphine. Unable to hold down food. Lacked an appetite. And the only thing keeping her from starving to death was the G-tube inserted into her abdomen.

They set up a hospital bed in the living room. A nurse visited once a day to tend to Caitlyn and administer a new morphine drip (since Nick's probation forbid him from handling prescription drugs).

Meg assumed all the household chores, took the girls out for ice cream and a movie that Saturday, handled calls and notes from friends and family, and sat alongside Caitlyn when it didn't obstruct caregivers. As Mary Lou correctly sensed, with the constant flux of traffic into the small home, Meg began to feel like an impediment. Especially when Mo never left Caitlyn's side.

Mo slept on the living room loveseat. Insisted everyone think positive. She even enlisted the help of a local group of charismatics to form a prayer circle around her ailing daughter and summon the healing powers of the Holy Spirit. And Meg knew, the moment Caitlyn started eating again, she'd find torn Jesus strips in her food.

Caitlyn saw little of her two daughters those first few weeks. When she wasn't knocked out on morphine, she suffered crippling abdominal pain. Each day the girls returned from school, Irene whisked them away so as not to disturb their mother. It was a heartbreaking reality Caitlyn had no choice but to accept at the moment.

After two weeks, Caitlyn felt guilty about Mo and Meg's help, especially with the shop teetering on bankruptcy and no one to look after it.

"You should go back," Caitlyn said. "I'll be fine."

"I'm not goin' anywhere," Mo said.

Caitlyn needed around-the-clock care as she prepared to embark on a debilitating regimen of chemo and radiation therapy. Nick's schedule of rehab meetings and sales calls (trying to generate some desperately needed income) prohibited him from assuming such a role. Had it not been for Caitlyn's disability insurance through the university, they'd be on the street.

A guilt-ridden Caitlyn insisted Mo return to Door County before she lost her shop and entire life savings.

"Those are just *things*," Mo kicked away the thought.

"That's your dream," Caitlyn felt horrible.

"You can always have dreams," Mo dismissed the notion with the brush of her hand. "I can't say the same about daughters."

Caitlyn appreciated Mo's words but still felt guilty. "Meg can run the shop."

Both Meg and Mo ruffled as if she suggested they jump off a cliff.

"Let her help," Caitlyn said. "She'll do a great job running it. She's so talented — "

" — Talented at gettin' into trouble," Mo scoffed. "The only thing she'll do is run me shop into the ground."

Meg retorted: "I think you did a good job of that yourself."

"Stop it!" Caitlyn rasped. "Please stop! I can't have you two fighting right now."

Both of them felt like two scolded children who knew they behaved badly.

"I have to get better for my girls," Caitlyn urged. "Please. If I'm going to beat this, I need both of you. You can't be fighting."

"What does it matter who's there," Mo brushed it away. "The bank plans to repossess it come Thanksgivin' anyway."

"Thanksgiving?" Meg said. "You had enough money to get to January."

"The bank called me note."

"What?" Meg and Caitlyn both exclaimed.

"Apparently Emmie Elefsson voiced her concern to some bankers about me shop not survivin', so they audited me books and called me note at the end of the month."

"Why didn't you tell us?" Meg said.

"Worryin' isn't goin' to change things," Mo turned her full attention on Caitlyn. "What matters right now is gettin' you better." Mo grabbed Meg's and Caitlyn's hand. "Take yer sister's hand," she instructed them both.

Linked in a triangle, Mo said a prayer and called upon the Blessed Virgin Mother to watch over her two daughters.

The next morning, Meg bid Caitlyn a heartfelt goodbye as she packed up the McCadillac to drive back to Door County, but not before Caitlyn made one last request.

"Talk to Robbie."

It gave Meg pause. Caitlyn embraced Meg's other hand and Meg smiled appreciatively as she felt her sister's love.

"Did you ever regret running off to Germany?" Meg asked.

"It seemed like the right thing to do at the time," Caitlyn reflected sadly.

Meg loved her sister dearly, and choked at the thought

of losing her. "I love you."

"I love you too."

The two sisters embraced with all their might, uncertain what the future held, neither wanting to let go of the other as tears welled in their eyes.

"Enough of this," Caitlyn wiped her eyes with a chuckle. "Alright, so this priest was holding confession one afternoon…"

Meg laughed. You could always count on Caitlyn for an Irish joke.

"…and this Irishman staggers into the church blind drunk. Stumbles down the aisle, bounces from pew to pew, crashes over a stack of prayer hymnals, then finally finds the confessional, goes in, and shuts the door. So the priest is sitting there, waiting for him to say something, and after about a minute or two, the priest clears his throat real loud so the man will know he's there and ready. Still nothing. Finally, the priest loses patience and bangs sharply on the wall three times…" *Knock, knock, knock*, Caitlyn rapped her hand. "…and the drunk fellow in the confessional says, 'It's no use knockin'…There's no toilet paper in here either!'"

They laughed.

CHAPTER 27

THE PIKEY

pikey—(pi -key) an Irish gypsy; a vagabond who constantly wanders to greener pastures; or literally, dirty thieving monkey-hybrids who live in caravans and crap in buckets

THE McCADILLAC PULLED UP to the front of the shop's rear gravel parking lot as dawn broke over the lake. Meg turned off the ignition and sat perfectly still, listening to the old engine rumble and knock for a good minute. Her head started to throb like the quadriceps of a marathoner running her last mile. Fast food wrappers and empty coffee cups littered the passenger side floor and seat. For the first time in 22 hours, she allowed her hands to release the steering wheel for more than a ten-minute rest stop.

Meg abandoned her life in Los Angeles and thanked her manager for everything.

The entire 1,300 miles passed in a high-octane mind race of angst, worry, sorrow, regret, and double shot mocha lattes, turning into an intense therapy session somewhere in upstate New York with her captive self as doctor and patient.

The vacant Irish shop rested alone in the quiet of winter's early gray light.

Down the hill, most of the sleepy stores remained in hibernation.

The lake remained perfectly still.

In the peacefulness of the breaking dawn, an exhausted Meg took it all in.

There was something special about this place. The summer she spent as a teenager remained the most magical of her life. Nary a time existed where she knew herself better or felt more complete. No other person evoked the best in her like Robbie. Nor elicited that freefalling fear of plummeting off a cliff.

With Robbie, she never controlled her emotions as she could with all others. It was unpredictable. Aggravating. Alive. Dangerous. Exhilarating.

No big-lights acting gig, or A-list party, or love affair made her feel as complete and happy as she did just sitting with Robbie on his boat surrounded by stinking fish.

She dissected her life the last 22 hours and felt empty.

The last decade, everything about her life was transient. She avoided serious commitments and believed in nothing other than herself.

She wanted to rekindle the 16-year-old girl of that summer years ago. The one who wasn't so cynical. The one who still took leaps of faith. Who still believed in love. She wanted to find that person again. And at that moment, she decided to do the scariest thing imaginable: commit to one place, in a steady job, and open herself to forming a permanent relationship.

She stared over the little village, no idea of the future or fate of Mo's shop. She just knew being here was the right thing. And knew the first local she needed to reach out to.

"Here, boy," Meg whistled, offering a fat carrot through the corral fence behind Al Johnson's. "No hard feelings. I'm sorry I hit you."

The lame goat stared at her.

"I'm glad to see you're walking around…well, limping. But hey, you know, lady goats might think that's sexy. Make you a little more mysterious."

The goat's ear twitched. He wasn't lured by the carrot.

"You look as alone as I do," Meg said. "I imagine you miss your roof. I don't blame you for still being mad at me. Why should you be different from anyone else in this town—and I hit you. Well, if you want it, it's yours." Meg tossed the carrot at him. "I'm really sorry."

Meg started to walk back to her car and heard a crunch. When she spun around, she saw Lars munching away.

"Maybe I should give the whole town carrots," Meg joked.

The next morning, merchants throughout downtown Whitefish Creek awoke to find a brown paper bag containing a fresh loaf of raisin bread outside their front door. No note. No marketing. Just a simple act of neighborly kindness with no agenda other than to do something nice. She even placed one in front of their biggest nemesis, Emmie Elefsson's Whitefish Creek Mercantile. And ironically, it was that act of kindness—the one Meg debated doing—that gave her the idea on how to save the shop.

CHAPTER 28

DANCING IN A CURRAGH

curragh—(cur-rok) a small canoe-like, Irish boat with a wooden frame over which animal hides are stretched; not very steady or safe; as the Irish saying goes: "God is good, but don't dance in a curragh (translation: don't tempt fate)

"YOU WILL IN ME HAT!" Mo forbid Meg.

"I'm doing it," Meg stood firm.

"Over me dead body!" Mo barked on the other end of the phone.

Meg smirked. "Don't you mean over mine?"

The only way to convince the bank to forestall any short sale or foreclosure was to find a reliable stream of substantive income. And there existed only one vacant position in all Door County paying that kind of money.

Meg discovered it on a forgotten old flier in the dusty corner of a vacant two-story white brick building. The store sat tucked further back from Main Street than its neighboring Whitefish Creek Mercantile, with a long cobblestone walk leading to its entrance. A sign out front read FOR SALE OR LEASE. A wooden sign above the door listed POST OFFICE. And in its dusty front window, taped decades ago on yellowed white paper, the faded stenciled words read: *Mail Carrier Wanted.*

Chairman Rufus E. Philpot laughed when Meg walked into his office and asked for the job.

"You do know every single mail carrier in Whitefish Creek died on the job," Chairman Philpot looked at her like she was a born idiot.

"I still want the job."

Chairman Philpot sat up in his desk. "Honey, no one with half the sense God gave a billy goat would want this job."

"Then think how popular you'll be. Not only will everyone get their mail, but you get to put a death curse on the Irish shop as well."

Chairman Philpot chuckled and they shook on it.

Mo insisted the lone Catholic priest on the northern peninsula, Father Brad Mohalski, bless the McCadillac before Meg embarked upon the cursed mail carrier position. She mailed a care package of lucky talismans (with strict orders to carry them in the vehicle at all times) that included a lucky rabbit's foot, a horseshoe, a cross, a blessed medal of the Virgin Mary, and a Triple-A card.

Meg awoke that first morning at the ungodly hour of 4 a.m., showered, brewed a large vat of coffee, arrived at the Main Street post office a little before 5 a.m., sorted mail for an hour, hopped in the Irish mobile that now bore an official U.S. Post Office license plate, clipped on her official Mail Carrier identification badge, and spent the rest of the morning delivering mail around the village of Whitefish Creek and its outlying cherry blossom fields and farmlands in her Irish flag on wheels.

She saw all kinds of wonderful places along the back roads of Door County. Old barns and farmhouses converted into artist galleries and studios. She met the loveliest Swedish couple who painted world-renown oil canvasses, and lived half the year in Door County and the other half in Germany. There was a great gay couple, Steven and Steve, who made intricate kites they shipped all over the world. Another woman made these funky metal twisty sculptures that apparently sold for ridiculous amounts of money. Gus Klinke ran an auto body repair shop from his barn, in addition to being Door County's premiere beekeeper. And one Finnish woman, Elsa Hedvig, the head chef at the Whitefish Creek Grill, was so excited about mail delivery (since it was difficult to run to Egg Harbor during business hours to retrieve letters from her family back in Finland), she left an open invitation for Meg to enjoy a free dinner.

Then there was the wooded piece of property with *Do Not Trespass* and *Beware of Dog* signs nailed to trees at its gravel road entrance, along with the rubber masks of several prominent Republican Presidents stuck on six foot spikes rising from the ground. But no curbside mailbox.

Wearily Meg crunched up the long gravel drive. A few hundred yards up, through the breaking bend of trees, a two-story wood cabin loomed on a hill with the most obnoxious, psychedelic paint-splashed chicken coop alongside it. The coop looked like a hippy commune for acid-dropping poultry.

Bam — *!* A shotgun blast fired across her bow.

"Jesus!" Meg slammed the brakes and hit the deck.

The McCadillac stalled out.

A man stumbled from the cabin, shotgun aimed at the driver's window, dressed in an old blue robe, sandals, and an oversized hunter's cap.

"Identify yourself!"

"I'm your postman," Meg nervously called from the pit of her seat.

"Postman?" the man said incredulously.

Meg collected herself and raised up a friendly handful of envelopes out the window. "I have your mail."

He lowered his shotgun and snatched the so-called "mail" from Meg's hand.

Meg peeked one eye out the window and watched her captor as he sifted through the letters. His bloodshot eyes and proverbial smirk under the hunter's cap were unmistakably Booker Wade.

Booker glanced up with a cackling smile. "Looks like you and I both have death wishes if you took this job. Thought I recognized the car. How's your mom?"

"Fine," Meg said, pulling herself up from the pit of the car seat and catching her breath. "You owe her for that shillelagh you lifted."

Booker grinned like a naughty boy. "I've been meaning to pay your mom a visit about that."

Meg smiled skeptically. "She's in Boston."

"Oh, yeah," Booker sobered. "I heard about your sister. I'm sorry."

"You heard about that?"

"Honey, you can't go to the john in this town without someone knowing how many squares of toilet paper you used. You tell your mom 'hi' from me," he grinned.

When Meg returned from her mail route and parked the Irish mobile in front of the neighboring Whitefish Creek Mercantile, Emmie Elefsson was fit to be tied. She tried to pass an ordinance against Irish vehicles, and when that failed, she forced the City to zone her front parking for Mercantile customers only. So Meg parked across the street, in full view of every customer leaving Emmie's store.

Meg held post office hours from noon to two, sorting new mail, issuing stamps, weighing packages, and meeting the incoming community. Everyone seemed so appreciative to no longer have to retrieve their mail at Egg Harbor, Meg ceased to be such the pariah and the Irish mobile became a welcome sight. One grateful local woman, Nattie Bjorklunden, brought Meg homemade apple butter cookies. Meg's split duties kept her so busy, she found no time to pay Robbie a visit. She hoped to hear his truck rumble down Main Street. Or see him walk into the post office or Irish shop. After a week of no Robbie, Meg drove to the fishing docks before she embarked on her postal route, and found Robbie's boat slip empty. None of the other fishermen reported seeing him in well over a month.

"I think he headed up to Canada," one old fisherman said.

"I think he headed south," said another. "Down to Panama."

"Panama?" Meg questioned, then drove by Robbie's home to find no sign of him.

The next day, Meg brought several loaves of Irish raisin bread into the post office. During those two hours, happy locals poured in and out, picking up their mail, swapping gossip, enjoying raisin bread, and sharing old stories about Whitefish Creek. One summerer-turned-year-round resident compared the post office's newfound communal atmosphere to the late Olga Wapple's general store. She recalled a time in her youth, back in the late 50s and early 60s, when the only phone in all of Whitefish Creek resided at the Wapple family General Store. Old Mrs. Wapple used to pin incoming messages on the front of her dress for the summer residents, like "Mrs. Hogan, your husband wants you to call him in St. Louis." And if you didn't come in that day, you'd get it the next day or the next, or someone you knew would invariably read the note on Mrs. Wapple's bosom and relay the message. No man ever missed a glance of Olga's billboard of a bosom.

Meg chatted with everyone, inquiring about Robbie's whereabouts, and heard everything from moved to Nova Scotia, joined the Canadian Coast Guard, to traversed the St. Lawrence Seaway to go fishing in Newfoundland. The only thing everyone agreed upon was that Robbie just shipped out one morning, said he needed to clear his head, and no one reported seeing him in almost two months.

CHAPTER 29

PAT-O-LANTERNS

'Tis better to sit on a pumpkin and have it all to yerself,
than be crowded on a velvet cushion.

—*Irish saying*

SCARECROWS APPEARED ALL over Main Street.

Two weeks before Halloween, straw men loitered outside every shop in Whitefish Creek. Big ones, fat ones, short ones, tall ones. Straw men. Straw women. Ones dressed like Vikings, another like Frankenstein. A witch, a pirate, a fairy with ginormous butterfly wings. Some depicted celebrities, others famous literary and movie characters. One mooned any passerby with two pumpkins for butt cheeks. But the grandest arrangement was outside the Whitefish Creek Mercantile.

Emmie Elefsson won Whitefish Creek's Annual Scarecrow Festival trophy the last nine years. She staged elaborate themes: one year a cast of twenty scarecrows recreated a scene from *Gone With The Wind*; another year she depicted the *Wizard of Oz*; and another year *Alice in*

Wonderland. This year was *Snow White and the Seven Dwarves* (with the evil witch, curiously enough, dressed in shamrock green).

Meg's contribution involved dressing a scarecrow in her red leprechaun outfit, which everyone mistook for a Christmas elf. But the shop remained open thanks to Meg's steady paycheck. And after she paid the mortgage, Meg gathered the other monthly bills, threw them into the air, and the ones that landed on her lap received payment. Those out of arms' reach returned to the bill basket for the next Pay Day Roulette.

The shop's balance sheet still carried the $1,200 deficiency from the gaunt elderly woman from Milwaukee who left with a bunch of Aran sweaters and the promise to mail a check now 90 days past due.

"Something more important probably distracted her," Mo reasoned over the phone, insisting she'd pay. Then she dictated strict instructions on decorating the shop for her favorite holiday.

Mo always insisted the Irish invented Halloween, explaining its origins arose from the ancient Celtic fire festival called "Samhain" (pronounced *sow-en*), which always took place on October 31st to mark the end of summer. On that single night of the year, Mo warned that recently disembodied spirits were allotted one last chance to remain on earth if they located a favorable body and possessed it. So villagers dressed in ghoulish costumes to make themselves so hideously unappealing that no spirit in its right mind would want them. They even paraded around the village making all kinds of ghastly noise to further dissuade any would-be possessors.

But of all the spooks who roamed that night, Mo loved to tell the story of Stingy Jack, a wicked drunkard Irish turnip farmer whose unrepentant life of debauchery was further enabled when he tricked the Devil into promising he'd never take his soul. When Jack died and God wanted no part of his wickedness, he humbly appeared at Hell's Gates only to have the Devil remind him of his coerced promise.

"But I have no place else to go," Jack groveled.

Then with a supercilious grin, the Devil told Jack that his spirit was cursed to roam the earth forever until he found an unsuspecting soul to possess and mend his ways. As the Devil threw Jack from Hell, he tossed Jack a single glowing ember from the eternal flames to help light his way through the cold darkness. Too hot to touch, Jack placed the ember in one of his hollowed-out turnips. Then cut holes to make a lantern and set his spirit wandering about the earth at night to find an unsuspecting soul. Folks who knew about Jack carved out turnips and placed candles inside to show, on the one night of the year he could possess someone, he'd find no unsuspecting soul in their house. People called them jack-o-lanterns. And when the Irish brought the tradition to America in the 1840s, they replaced turnips with the more abundant and easier-to-carve American vegetable: pumpkins.

Mo still remained steadfast to the original tradition of turnips, and insisted Meg undertake the laborious task of carving the hard, hollowless vegetables (which smelled something awful when left indoors with a lit candle) that Mary Lou dubbed "Pat-o'-lanterns."

When the sun dropped on Halloween, Mo instructed

Meg to turn off all the lights and fill the house with lit candles. And if a flame ever turned blue, Mo swore a ghost lurked nearby.

Meg remained true to Mo's long-distance wishes. The days leading up to Halloween, she offered customers "lambs wool"—roasted, crushed apples mixed in milk—and a taste of the traditional Halloween culinary fare "colcannon"—mashed taters, parsnips, and chopped onions. For the sweet tooth, she served Barmbrack—fruit cake with a piece of a rag, a coin, and a ring baked inside. Irish tradition held if a person's slice of cake contained the ring, it promised impending romance or good luck. A piece of the rag portended a gloomy financial future. And the coin promised a prosperous year.

Meg's slice contained the rag.

When trick-or-treaters knocked on the shop's door, Meg handed out traditional Irish soul cakes (square pieces of bread with currants that obligated the recipient to say prayers for the donor's deceased relatives in limbo).

"Happy Halloween," Meg smiled, as the disgruntled children eyed the unwanted treats like Charlie Brown's rocks. And before they exited the porch, Meg splashed a fistful of salt in their hair, claiming it protected them against the night's evil spirits. Needless to say, the moment she shut the door, she heard a lot of the unwanted soul cakes flung back at the shop.

Meg followed Mo's instructions to the letter. If she wanted salt thrown in kids' hair after dropping some religious treat in their sack, far be it for Meg to mess with Irish tradition.

"That's what makes us unique," Mo insisted, reiterating her reason for starting the shop: "Spreadin' Irish tradition."

Halloween marked the last hoorah in Whitefish Creek. Most shops along Main Street closed for the winter in the ensuing days. And those that remained kept winter hours. After that first week of November, the entire place felt like a ghost town. No more customers. No boats on the lake. Even fishermen shut down the entire month of November to allow the whitefish a chance to spawn.

The weather grew frigid. The only activity in the lakeside villages centered around the pubs. Even Meg's postal route shortened by half, with the last of the diehard summerers returning home for the winter.

Three weeks passed and no Robbie. She made subtle inquiries during post office hours, but no one knew the specifics about his absence.

The third Sunday, Meg used the Fitzgibbons's boat and motored out to Plum Island in the cold air to seek Door County's resident hermit. She designed a dress especially for Alma and placed it in the shop's nicest gift bag.

"I brought you a gift."

Alma stood in the doorway staring at her with those expressionless dark eyes.

"It's a dress. I made it myself. Designed it just for you."

Alma grabbed the bag without ado.

"I thought you might look nice in it. I wasn't sure if you had any dresses…"

Alma said nothing, glanced at the bag, then shut the door, ending the awkward encounter.

A few days later Meg sat in the shop, knitting a hat,

when she noticed a black-haired pumpkin of a head outside the front window.

Meg opened the front door with a *jing-a-ling-ling* to find Alma standing in the cold wearing her dress. Seeing her on the mainland was rare enough, but seeing her in anything other than dark pants and sweaters was a first.

Alma hoisted a dead bird with its webbed feet clutched in her fist. "Seagull meat," she said in her monotone 'sconsin accent. "Tastes good wid potatoes, ay."

"Oh, thank you," Meg smiled.

Alma shrugged. It was just meat. Then turned to depart.

"Wait!" Meg said.

Alma stopped and turned.

"Do you know where Robbie is?"

Alma stared at her with those dark expressionless eyes. "On his boat."

Meg grinned. "Do you know where his boat is?"

Alma shrugged. "Somewhere on the water I s'pose." She began to walk off.

"Wait! Please. Come in. Are you hungry? You can show me how to prepare it."

With little words, Alma marched inside and showed how to prepare a nice seagull stew with chopped potato slices. Then they sat at the coffee table at the downstairs hearth while Meg brewed up a pot of Irish tea (with a generous blend of whiskey).

"You look great in that dress," Meg said.

The compliment failed to register with Alma as another painful lull set in until Alma spoke. "My barn's fixed. Robbie finished fixin' it 'bout two months ago."

The mention of Robbie brought Meg hope. "Did Robbie ever say anything about leaving?"

"Said you left."

"My sister had cancer," Meg said. "Stomach cancer. My mother's back with her in Boston. That's why I'm here. To run the shop."

Another lull. Alma showed no reaction.

"My sister's going through chemo right now," Meg said. It felt good to talk about it. "I can't stop worrying about her. She has two little girls…"

"We all gotta die sometime," Alma said monotone.

The hermit's insensitive words stunned Meg. "Caitlyn's not going to die."

Alma grunted. "My father died of lung cancer. Coughed up blood one night. Two months later he died. I was ten."

Alma finished her tea, and without a word, stood and walked out, leaving Meg with the harsh reality of Caitlyn's predicament.

A bit later, the front door opened and closed with its *ring-a-ling-ling.*

Meg walked into the foyer to find a blond-haired Amazon standing at the counter.

Anna's eyes honed in on her as Meg froze. "You came back."

"Do you know where Robbie is?" Meg asked.

Anna prowled towards her like a lioness to its kill, sizing her up, then grinned, knowing she held the upper hand. "Tomorrow morning. Ten 'til five. We'll talk then."

"Ten 'til five?" Meg questioned the ridiculous hour. "I have postal duties. Let's talk now."

"Ten 'til five. I'm only honking once. And wear warm clothes."

"Why don't you just tell me where you want to meet and I'll be there?"

"You think I'd be caught dead anywhere near your crazy Irish car?" Anna shook her head, annoyed, and started for the door. As she stepped outside, Meg thought she heard Anna utter the slur of all Northern Wisconsin slurs: "FISH."

CHAPTER 30

TURKEYS

There are three creatures beyond ruling—
a turkey, a pig, and a women.

—*Irish saying*

THE NEXT MORNING at 4:50 a.m., Robbie's Northern
Lights Fishing truck pulled outside the shop and honked.
Meg's heart leapt until she saw Anna alone in the driver's
seat, decked out in camouflage.

"Come on," Anna demanded.

Meg wore jeans, a cream Irish fisherman's sweater, knit
hat and brown designer jacket.

"What is that?" Anna disapproved of her outfit, reaching
into the back. "I thought as much." She pulled out a bundle
of camouflage. "Put this on over your clothes."

"Why?"

"Just do it."

"I don't see why we have to do all this to talk — "

" — Do you want to know where Robbie is?"

Twenty minutes later, they drove down a dirt road and

stopped at a wooded alcove under the pitch-black sky, where Anna cut the engine and walked to the rear of the truck.

"What are we doing?" Meg questioned, dressed in camouflage pants and jacket.

Anna reappeared with a shotgun.

Meg startled.

"Don't want to scare away the turkeys," Anna said. "Let's go. We need to get to our spot before the sun breaks."

Meg sat idly, confused as Anna rolled her eyes in exasperation and spoke slowly as if explaining to a kindergartner. "It's the first day of turkey season."

"Well then shouldn't I have one of those?" Meg pointed to Anna's shotgun.

"You don't have a permit."

"Yeah, but shouldn't I have one, you know, just in case."

"In case what? We get ambushed by turkeys? You ever shoot anything before?"

"No."

"Ever fire a shotgun?"

"No."

"Here," Anna reached into her coat pocket. "Hold out your hand."

"What?"

"Just hold out your hand."

Meg reluctantly acquiesced and felt her hand fill with seeds. "Corn?" Meg stared at the dried kernels.

"Yeah," Anna grinned. "If one of those monsters charges, throw it. That'll keep 'em off ya."

Meg felt stupid.

Anna laughed as she headed into the dark thicket.

"Where's Robbie?" Meg started to fear Anna buried him in the backwoods.

Meg looked around at the wintry darkness and eerie ground fog that covered the forest. Not another soul around. Then decided that staying with She-Viking seemed safer than waiting alone.

When Meg caught up, Anna began to talk.

"I was a struggling single mom when I met Robbie. Never finished high school. I thought my ceiling in life was waiting tables at the Hitching Post. Robbie was the one who encouraged my interest in wines. He used to come in and order a beer, and I'd always be talking everyone's ear off about our latest wine selections, how to taste it, what to eat with it, why—all this stuff. The owner let me order all our selections. Not that we were that upscale. But I got some real good ones. And actually turned a bunch of brat-eating-beer-chugging cheese heads into wine drinkers. So when Robbie told me about his idea for the cherry orchard and offered to fly me out to California for a year to learn about winemaking, it was the nicest thing anyone's ever done for me. He gave me a career. Helped me raise my daughter," she smiled fondly. "He was my knight in shining ar — " Anna abruptly stopped, her hand halting Meg as she listened intently to the woods. Slowly, she crept into the brush trying not to make a sound.

"I saw a big tom around here the other day," Anna whispered. "They must roost somewhere in those trees," she pointed to a thick grove of pines about forty yards away.

Anna glanced up at the emerging twilight. "Sun will be out soon. We can hide in this brush," she pointed to a muddy swamp of fallen trees, wet leaves, and thorny brush. The perfect place to hide a body.

"Why can't we just hide behind one of those trees?"

"Do you have any idea what we're up against?" Anna exclaimed quietly. "Imagine a creature with the eyes of an eagle, the super hearing of a dog, and the cleverness of a raccoon. If these beasts had any ability to smell, we wouldn't have a chance. Now get down. And stay absolutely quiet. No moving. No talking. They hear one sound, it's over. They'll high tail out of here and never come back."

"Why did you take me out here if all we're going to do is keep our mouths shut?"

"Scoot over," Anna nudged.

"Where's Robbie?"

"Keep your voice down," Anna whispered. She scanned the grove of trees with her rifle ready. Her voice spoke in measured whispers to blend with the wind. "I thought he'd be back by now. He's never missed turkey season. We always go together," her words bore a hint of remorse.

Anna dug into her pocket and fished out a small wooden box with a sliding top.

"What's that?" Meg asked.

"Turkey call," Anna hushed, drawing the small box to her lips and blew. *Yelp.*

"That doesn't sound anything like a turkey," Meg expected *gobble, gobble.*

"It's a strut," Anna whispered.

"A what?"

Anna gritted her teeth. "Strut. A hen's mating call."

"Don't you mean 'slut'?" Meg grinned.

Anna looked exasperated. She blew again. *Yelp*.

The next thirty minutes crept like hours. Meg's ADD leg started bouncing. "Can I try?"

"Shhh!" Anna whispered. "You gotta know how to make a strut sound. Otherwise, it can sound like a cluck, or gobble, or even worse. A pok."

"Pok?" Meg asked. "What's a pok?"

Anna grabbed Meg's restless leg and stilled it. "Pok is turkey for 'Get the hell out of here.'"

"I say we pok," Meg said. "We've been here over an hour and you still haven't told me where Robbie is."

"Shhh!" Anna urged.

"No! I'm sick of shhhing. I'm sick of waiting for turkeys that are never going to appear. My backside's soaked. I'm cold. I'm hungry. I'm bored. And I'm sick of playing this game. Either tell me where Robbie is or don't! Shoot me or don't! But hell if I'm gonna sit here and let you screw with me!" Meg shot straight up.

Twenty yards away a big tom stared straight at her.

Meg stared back speechless.

And from the bushes all around…

Pok — ! Pok — ! Pok — ! Pok — ! Pok — ! followed by the frantic rustle of retreating turkeys and what sounded like sheets flapping on a clothesline.

Anna's jaw dropped in exasperation.

Meg froze at the realization, then gradually, a slight apologetic smile appeared as she turned to Anna and saw her eyes shooting poisonous daggers at her.

When they finally marched back to the car, Anna refused to speak.

"I didn't know they were there," Meg said.

Anna reached the truck without a word.

"I told you I didn't want to come in the first place. We could've just talked back at the shop..."

"No! You don't understand. Robbie loves turkey season. He loves the Door. When you left, I've never seen him so distant. He called off our wedding. Loaded up his boat with supplies and headed towards I don't know where. He said he needed to get away from everything and everyone and just think. Then he said something about traveling the St. Lawrence Seaway, maybe up to Newfoundland or down to Panama. That was back in August. I don't even know if he's alive."

Anna stared silently into the woods for the longest time, and Meg knew not to say a word. Finally, Anna turned back to Meg and spoke with quiet regret. "I accepted a job offer at a small winery in Sonoma County."

"You what?" Meg asked, startled. "What about the winery here?"

"I already have a replacement. Donnie Kodanko. He's been my understudy the last few years. Very capable."

"Does Robbie know?"

"He knows. My daughter's been wanting to get out of the Door for a while. She wants to pursue a career in music. She likes the idea of San Francisco. California would be good for her. She's never quite fit in around here. I've been putting it off because of everything with the winery...and Robbie. It's not fair to her anymore."

Anna stared at Meg intently. "You've always been a wall between Robbie and I. You know that. I thought I could break through it. I kept telling myself year after year he just needed time. I even tried to convince myself that would be enough. Then you show back up. And I see you two, how you act with one another..." she trailed off. "He's never looked at me the way he does you," Anna said bravely. "I can't compete with that. I shouldn't have to. So, the only other choice I have..."

Anna cocked her rifle at Meg.

"Jesus!" Meg jumped.

Anna laughed, lowering her rifle. "I'm just messing with you. Relax."

Meg breathed a sigh.

"He's yours," Anna conceded. "I'm setting him free, as the saying goes. If you love someone, right? See if they come back."

"The annual Lutefisk eating contest is in a few weeks," Anna noted. "Robbie's never missed defending his title. I'm guessing he'll be back then. Figure out what you want in life. Because if it's not Robbie, or you're still not sure, don't be here when he gets back. You owe him that."

CHAPTER 31

THE SUPREME LUTEFISK

The greatest love—the love above all loves,
even greater than that of a mother...
is the tender, passionate, undying love,
of one beer drunken slob for another.

—Irish love ballad

DECEMBER 1ST OFFICIALLY ENDED the six-week moratorium on commercial fishing in the Door, kicking off what local fishermen aptly dubbed Viking Season (the trifecta of harsh winter months: December, January, and February). Cold and snow roared off the lake. Layers of icy spray froze heavily enough on boats to capsize them. Crewmembers stoked large coal-burning furnaces to keep warm. Fishing vessels faced the morning task of ramming through several hundred yards of freshly frozen harbor to reach open waters.

Every year, on the eve of the season, fishermen displayed their fortitude by gathering for the Sons of Norway Lutefisk and Meatball Dinner to "get their inner-Viking on."

They threw down shots of the high-octane Nordic liquor aquavit. Dined on the toxic gelatinous rotting cod lutefisk. And the toughest of the brethren pitted their iron stomachs against one another in the northern peninsula's most popular annual event: the Lutefisk Eating Contest. The atmosphere felt every bit as electric as a heavyweight title bout. Villagers packed in elbow-to-elbow, drinking buckets of beer, taking bets, anxiously waiting to see who claimed this year's $5,000 top prize and the exalted title of Supreme Lutefisk (which on more than one occasion resulted in rushing some poor retching contestant to the ER). All part of the fun.

The sold-out event took place at the Whitefish Creek Grill.

The rules were simple. One hour. All the lutefisk you gagged down. The current Door County record stood at just over seven pounds (the world record at eight). And they imposed a retention rule, requiring the winner to keep down his lutefisk for a mandatory fifteen minutes before making an outhouse run.

Only the bravest of the brave dared step into the spotlight of this high-stakes, high-pressure, highly esteemed contest. There were certain expectations. Certain unspoken qualifications. You couldn't be some half-baked local yokel with delusions of grandeur. This was first-class. Which is why the entire peninsula gasped when, for the first time in the contest's 80-year history, a FISH entered her name.

At first it was just a stunt. Partly born out of Meg's boredom. Partly to stir publicity. Partly to see Robbie's expression of sheer shock—if he showed up. But not without hope of winning the desperately needed $5,000 cash prize. And Meg concocted the most deliciously diabolical strategy to claim Robbie's long-held title. Sweet payback for that summer fourteen years earlier when his prank subjected her to a miserable night of lutefisk's revenge.

Emmie Elefsson and her Door County Historical Society minions denounced Meg's eligibility. "It's unprecedented," Emmie was quoted in the *Door Countian*. "She's not a Door Countian. She's not a Wisconsinite. She's certainly no Son of Norway. And she's not a lutefisk eater. We can't allow the McKennas to undermine anymore fabrics of our community."

After a long deliberation, the Supreme Lutefisk Commission sheepishly admitted no rule on the books forbade it, and conceded: "The lutefisk is as lutefisk does."

The whole peninsula buzzed with whispers and disapprovals. More than a few locals secretly enjoyed watching the contest shaken up from its traditionally all male cast. And a news crew from Green Bay drove up to interview the groundbreaking contestant.

People lined up outside to buy tickets. Meg's entry created such controversy that it fast became the largest attended event in the contest's 80-year history. Only the question of Robbie's participation remained. And the morning of the competition, his boat slip sat empty.

By five o'clock that evening, Wisconsinites packed the Whitefish Creek Grill, anxiously awaiting the hopeful arrival of the reigning champ amidst the usual pageantry of comers: one sported a T-shirt that read REAL MEN EAT LUTEFISK; another wore a Superman shirt and cape; another sported full Viking regalia with rock-star sunglasses;

another dressed like Vegas Elvis in a white-sequined jumpsuit; one a Packers' jersey and cheese head; and the rest pretty much wore coveralls.

Meg shamelessly wore a homemade blue T-shirt that advertised in big green letters All Things Irish, which she let hang loosely over her waistline to hide the new muffin top that prevented her from squeezing into her skinny jeans. Since Caitlyn's diagnosis, she found comfort in potato chips and buttered popcorn.

Several local news cameras staked their spots in the packed room.

Chairman Philpot directed Meg to the end of the long link of tables next to Robbie's empty chair, providing a necessary gap between Meg and the other contestants who refused to sit next to the "pretender."

"It's time for da lutefisk, ay," Chairman Philpot announced.

A rumble from the back of the restaurant turned into applause and cheers as an unmistakable figure parted the crowd with his green ball cap, flannel shirt, coveralls, and a mangy beard and mustache.

"Our reigning champion," Chairman Philpot cheered.

Robbie stepped front and center to the applause of all, offered a wave, glanced at Meg, revealing neither shock nor surprise, and took the empty seat.

"Nice beard," Meg tried to break the ice.

"Another one of your publicity stunts?" Robbie grumbled at her presence.

"I was just hungry," Meg grinned. "Thought I'd grab a bite."

Robbie smirked at the ludicrous notion. "If I remember correctly, last time you ate lutefisk you spent a night on the toilet."

Just then, assistants set plates carrying nine pounds of the gray jellyfish-like glob before each contestant and Meg mustered every bit of strength to keep from retching as she mugged for the cameras.

Chairman Philpot stood center stage to welcome the contestants and crowd.

"If everyone will stand and join me in da lutefisk national anthem."

The whole place silenced, stood, and reverently placed their hands over their hearts—Meg followed their lead—and to the tune of *O Tennenbaum*, sang:

"O Lutefisk, O Lutefisk, how fragrant your aroma,
O Lutefisk, O Lutefisk, you put me in a coma.
You smell so strong, you look like glue,
You taste just like an old shoe,
But lutefisk, come Saturday, I think I'll eat you anyway.

"O Lutefisk, O lutefisk, I put you in the doorway.
I wanted you to ripen up just like they do in Norway.
A dog came by and sprinkled you.
I hit him with my overshoe.
O lutefisk, now I suppose, I'll eat you while I hold my nose.

"O Lutefisk, O lutefisk, you have a special flavor.
O Lutefisk, O lutefisk, all good Norwegians savor.

That slimy slab we know so well

Identified by ghastly smell.

O lutefisk, O lutefisk, our loyalty won't waver."

Wild applause erupted.

Chairman Philpot beamed with delight, and as the contestants retook their seats and readied their game faces, he let out a whopping: "Let the lutefisk begin!"

Someone blew an air horn and the contestants dove in like pigs to a trough, choking down the rancid fish oil and toxic lye that seemed in rigorous competition to see which could render the dish more inedible.

Meg paced herself like a tortoise, hoping the large bottle of Pepto Bismo she chugged coated her stomach like a flack jacket.

About twenty minutes into the frenzy, Robbie and several contestants broke from the pack. The rest slowed.

"So you ventured outside the Door?" Meg asked Robbie between chews. "Where'd you go?"

Robbie tried to ignore her, shoveling another forkful when to his surprise, his stomach grumbled uneasily.

"That doesn't sound good," Meg said.

Robbie dismissed the gurgle and resumed eating.

"So I heard you went to Canada?"

From the other end of the table, one of the contestants stood, holding his gut, and quickly scooted to the bathroom, abandoning all title hopes.

Right on schedule, Meg grinned.

At the thirty-minute mark, the frontrunners approached four pounds, Meg reached half a pound, and the rest hit a wall. Forks lifted slower. Throats tightened. Heavy sweat poured off their brows. Then Elvis's stomach gurgled. His face contorted, and a sick grumble sent him bolting for the john.

Meg grinned again. Just as planned.

Grrrrrraaauuu, Robbie's emoting stomach gave him pause. Another contestant bolted for the latrine.

"What did you do?" Robbie noted Meg's devilish grin.

Meg smiled at him. "Funny thing about this contest. Do you know there are no specific rules how the lutefisk is prepared? None at all."

"What did you do?" Robbie suspected the worst.

"Well, as it turns out, Elsa, the chef here, is from Norway. Her whole family's back there. Very remote town. They don't have Internet or anything. So the only way they can communicate with each other is through the old U.S. Mail. I can't tell you how excited she was when I took over the postal duties here. With her hours, she always had so much trouble finding time to get down to Egg Harbor's post office. Now it comes right to her door."

"What did you do?" Robbie demanded, fearing her response.

"Well, when I told her I was in the contest, she was more than happy to accommodate my request of giving all the lutefisk an extra soaking of lye and keeping it swimming in grease."

Grrrrrraaaaaoorrrrr, Robbie's stomach rumbled. "Oh God."

"Yeah, that really doesn't sound good. Looks like Viking guy down there's giving you a run for your money."

Viking guy eyed Robbie with a competitive fervor from the other end of the table, shoveling more and more toxic stink into his mouth.

"Better start eating if you want to keep your title," Meg beamed.

"I hate you," Robbie said, muscling down a heap of double-toxic greasy sludge.

Meg took another small bite. "Bon appetite."

More contestants abandoned their posts with wrenching, gurgling stomachs.

With ten minutes left, Meg, Robbie, Viking Guy and Superman remained the last four standing.

The two other competitors pressed Robbie to eat more, closing in on seven belt-loosening pounds.

"So tell me about Canada," Meg grinned.

"I'm not talking to you," Robbie said, forcing down another stomach-turning bite. *Grrrrrroooaaaaa.*

"Yeah, that just sounds wrong," Meg teased. "You know, that's another interesting thing about the rules. You can't make an outhouse run for fifteen minutes after the contest ends or you're disqualified. Fifteen long minutes."

Gggrrrrooooooooaaaaaaaaaarrrrrraaaa..., Superman's stomach silenced the room. He let out an "Oh God," and bolted for the pot, making it about three-fourths through the crowd when everyone shuddered at a loud gastric explosion.

"Oooo, he didn't make it," Meg grinned. "How embarrassing. Five minutes left. Better keep eating. Viking Guy's pulling ahead."

"I really hate you," Robbie said.

Giant beads of sweat dripped off Robbie's and Viking

Guy's uncomfortable faces. They looked green. Their ears were bright red. Both competitors lifted their forks as if drudging hundred pound weights, determined to match the other bite-for-bite, while their stomachs gurgled and churned in vehement protest.

"You look really green," Meg said. "And your ears are beet red. I don't think I've ever seen you sweat so much."

Robbie concentrated on keeping his stomach from mutiny.

"You know another interesting rule about this contest," Meg continued. "All you need to do is eat a pound of lutefisk to qualify for the money. So what's so funny, if the two of you can't hold it down for fifteen minutes, guess who wins?"

The revelation hit Robbie like a deer in headlights as the final air horn blew.

"That's it," Chairman Philpot signaled. "Forks down!"

The judges quickly swooped in to remove the plates and weigh them.

"You don't look good," Meg noted.

Robbie winced at a sharp pain in his gut. Fat beads of sweat rolled off his pale face. His mouth puckered sourly. A nauseous Viking Guy eyed him, waiting to see if he'd bow out.

"So tell me about your trip," Meg delighted. "I'm so impressed you finally left the Door."

Viking Guy's stomach made a horrible sound. Then Robbie's, as he put his hands on the side of his gut and took hard measured breaths to keep everything in.

"Sounds like that lutefisk wants out — " Meg grinned,

Grrrrooaaa, her stomach betrayed her.

Robbie raised his pained brow with a grin.

"I'm fine." Meg's stomach rumbled again.

"You sound fine," Robbie grinned, then doubled over with a loud *grrooaaa*.

Viking Guy clutched his gut. "What's the weight?" he groaned at Chairman Philpot. "Did I beat him?"

"It's not official until fifteen minutes after," Chairman Philpot stated.

"Tell us!" the two rivals winced in agony as their legs tied into a pretzel to keep from exploding.

"Knudson by a tenth of a pound," Chairman Philpot took pity, and Viking Guy bolted for the bathroom with Robbie longing to be him.

A loud gastric explosion erupted in the crowd.

"He didn't make it either," Meg grinned. "Looks like it's you and me, fish boy."

Robbie's stomach made the longest unworldly sound that contorted his face into a knot. Robbie clinched, trying to hold in whatever God-awful intestinal volcano threatened to erupt.

Meg stepped away, fearing what horror she planted.

"The St. Lawrence Seaway," Robbie winced.

"What?"

"I went through the St. Lawrence Seaway," Robbie gritted in pain. "To the Atlantic. Down the southern coast. Past Cuba. To Central America. Through the Panama Canal…"

"You went through the Panama Canal?" Meg couldn't believe it.

"…Up Central America. Then Mexico. California. To Los Angeles."

"You went to look for me?" Meg was overwhelmed, then a loud *grrrrooooa* doubled her over. "Oh God," she clinched.

Robbie slowly stood, his bleary, sallow eyes fixated on the restroom at the far end of the restaurant, calculating its distance, gauging his chances…

Ggrrrrooooooaaaaa — "Oh God!" he darted for the latrine like a soldier out of a grenade-infested foxhole.

But before Meg could gloat…*Grrooaaa* — she doubled over, grimacing as her sphincter twitched like a jumping bean and sent her rushing for relief.

A line outside the ladies room blocked Meg's entry; so she charged into the men's and darted into the first open stall.

Robbie groaned from the adjoining stall. They both started laughing hysterically at their predicament, interrupted by "Oh God," and gastric explosions.

And at that moment, affixed to neighboring toilets, in all its unglamorous, raw, embarrassing imperfection, Meg rediscovered true love.

CHAPTER 32

THE LIGHTHOUSE

It is easy to be pleasant when life flows like a song,
but the test of the heart is trouble,
and it always comes along.

—*Irish saying*

ROBBIE SURPRISED MEG AT sunset as Lighthouse Island appeared off the bow.

The tower's lantern room peeked out from the island's treetops. Its new, silver framework gleamed in the setting sun. The tiny island's sandy shoreline was now manicured. Pristine white sands replaced the pasture of unfettered sea grass she remembered. And nestled amongst the cedars at the base of the light tower rested the quaint, one-story keeper's cottage. Its red roof looked newly shingled. The once-peeling sallow outside walls shone a crisp white. The chipped, yellowing window frames were now stripped and polished into a rich dark oak.

It looked like she always dreamed.

Over the last fourteen years, she romanticized about it

from time to time. Let her mind escape to this place whenever she needed comfort.

She glanced back to the wheelhouse and knew by Robbie's smile that he was the architect behind this.

Robbie cut the engine as *The Osprey* coasted up against the refurbished wooden dock.

"Grab a line," he signaled Meg.

Meg broke her gaze and grabbed a rope, as Robbie walked up to one of the dock's posts and pulled them closer.

"Tie us up," he smiled and Meg obliged.

"You did this?" Meg asked.

Robbie grinned. "I had the chance to buy it about ten years ago."

"You bought it?" Goosebumps prickled her body.

"Here," Robbie helped secure the rope to the dock.

"It looks amazing," Meg admired.

"It's still a work in progress. I had to have an outfit up East make the tower."

Robbie stepped onto the dock, and Meg followed him to the lighthouse.

Inside was no longer covered in dirt. Albeit a little dusty. Several walls were opened up, revealing new 2 x 4 frames and some electrical wiring. A few tools were scattered on the floor.

"I've been doing the wiring. It took forever to run an electric cable out here. I just got running water."

While Robbie lit some logs in the fireplace, Meg meandered into the bedroom and delighted at the sight of the old black-and-white keeper's picture hanging on the wall. Fourteen years ago, the picture was eerily clean amidst the inch of dust that covered everything else, causing them to speculate that it was the work of his widow's ghost.

"You kept the picture," Meg approved of the pristine frame.

"Didn't seem right to get rid of it. I don't think the old keeper would approve even if I wanted to."

"Did you see her?" Meg's brown eyes twinkled deliciously at the thought of a ghost story. "You did, didn't you."

Robbie grinned. "I don't know what I saw."

"Tell! Tell!"

"Well, I'm still not sure. It was late. I was probably punchy. I just finished tearing down the old light tower. And I was standing right there, in the kitchen. About where you are now. And out the corner of my eye, I saw my hammer float across the room, real slow, like this — "

" — No way."

"Then it just—wham. Sped up and slammed into the wall."

"Oh my gosh. For real?"

"I think she was mad I tore down the tower. I didn't come back for two months. And the night I finished the new frame, I was maybe a hundred yards away on my boat, not even, and I looked back, and saw a faint light in the tower. I don't know if I was tired, or it was some reflection from the moon, or what. But I swear I saw the figure of a woman staring out at me."

"Oooo, that gives me chills," Meg said, delighted. She gazed deeply at the whiskered face of the boy she fell in love with years ago. The only boy she ever loved.

Meg felt her breath stop as she melted into his penetrating blue eyes. Her body went numb as he leaned in, then she pulled away.

Robbie looked confused.

Meg smiled cautiously. "What about Anna and Riley? They left because of me."

"They left because of _me_. We were a family for Riley's sake. And it worked. For all of us. Now Riley's grown up. She's ready for bigger places. She's been ready for a while. And Anna and I…If that was right, it would've worked long ago. Both of us realized that."

"How do you know this won't work out?"

"What do you want me to say? How ever since that summer, sometimes, when I'm alone on my boat, I still hear your voice making fun of me. Or how I could never forget how you'd look at me with that guilty crooked grin any time a fish flopped out of your hands back into the lake. Or how I've spent the last decade fixing up this island because it was the only place that still let me feel close to you. Why do you think it's taken so long? I knew the moment I finished, Anna wanted to get married here, and it would all end. Us. What _we_ shared."

Their long-held feelings for each other tingled in the air. Robbie's gentle lips touched hers.

She had forgotten their softness. How perfect they felt.

His calloused fingers reached out ever so gently, slowly tracing down the length of her arm, the curve of her hip, rediscovering her. All of her.

Her fine arm hairs stood on end as he brushed over her with a longing that sent an electric charge through her body.

She closed her eyes and parted her lips, relishing the sensation of his hand on her body.

His caress lingered at her wrist, the tip of his index finger and thumb sliding around its tiny circumference with the care of handling the most precious crystal, refamiliarizing himself with its beguiling slenderness.

She felt his other hand on her hip. He admired its curve, tracing upwards, thumb hooking under the end of her shirt to lift it ever so slightly and feel flesh on flesh.

Her entire body tingled.

An overwhelming rush of feelings flooded her.

Her heart quickened as his fingers moved over her, lingering to trace the tiny mole next to her belly button.

He wanted to savor every part of her, down to the smallest detail. And she wanted him to know her again.

The two separated lovers gazed longingly at one another until the past fourteen years evaporated. It seemed as not a day had passed since they last embraced.

He kissed her softly on the neck, then the lips. She felt the welcome moisture of his mouth and the faint taste of cherries. He was more muscular than she remembered as their bodies pressed against one another.

The intense feelings Meg suppressed from 14 years ago flooded forward. They needed their skin to touch one another. And then that wasn't close enough. She needed to feel him inside her.

Fourteen years of lost passion erupted in what was so tender and perfect. A piece of themselves had been missing all those years, and for the first time since that summer, they felt complete again.

They could not hold each other long enough, and when it ended, they lay in the other's arms, basking in a happiness they only remembered.

Robbie finally spoke. "You have funny toes," Robbie said as he explored them.

Meg glanced down at her feet extending from the covers. "No I don't."

"Your middle toe is longer than the others. Look," he held up her foot.

"So."

"That's not normal. Look at mine. See how they curve. Yours go straight across. Like Fred Flintstone feet."

"They are not," Meg slapped him playfully, pulling away her foot.

"They are," Robbie chuckled. "You have Flintstone feet."

Meg hit him again as she tucked her feet under the covers.

"Don't hide. I have to see those things again," he ferreted out her toes.

"Will you stop," she yanked her foot away and they both shared a laugh. Then they began to kiss one another until they made love again. This time slowly, savoring every movement and touch.

They talked late into the night and early morning, finally falling asleep in each other's arms.

Meg awoke from that deep Door County slumber in a puddle of drool, with warm morning light shining through the window. She felt completely relaxed under the covers. She stretched until her joints cracked and then reached for

Robbie with a blissful smile...

A green, book-size present with an orange bow lay in his stead. Meg grinned. She liked presents. But she wondered where Robbie was.

She reached over and opened the white card on top; and inside, written in Robbie's terrible penmanship:

> *Went to grab breakfast and coffee.*
> *Sleep in. You like sleep. Be back soon.*
> *Love, Robbie.*

> *Yes, you can open it.*

Meg beamed. He knew her well.

Meg tore open the green wrapping paper to expose an elegant, leather-bound sketchbook and a box of sharpened pencils.

Warmth poured through her body like the welcome uplift of sunlight. Her heart fluttered.

She never owned an actual artist's sketchbook before. She always scribbled her fashion ideas in lined notebooks or scraps of paper (when she used to design). The creative impulse inside her still sparked with a new fashion idea every now and then (that never quite died), but she hadn't put pen to paper in years.

As she admired the sketchbook, it felt like seeing a dear friend.

Slowly, she opened its exquisite binding.

Her breath caught.

Inside lay the stained sketch of Svea Knudson's dress

that Meg presented Robbie almost fifteen years earlier.

Meg beamed. She couldn't wait for her Richard Joyce to return. And as she basked in the moment, somewhere ingrained in her mind, echoed the unsettling feeling of her mother's crazy Good Day Bad Day Theory: whenever something good happened in life, something worse lurked just around the corner.

Meg hated Mo's Irishisms.

CHAPTER 33

BEAN SIDHE

'Tis an Irishman's abiding sense of tragedy which
sustains him through temporary periods of joy.

—*Irish saying*

MEG MCKENNA PULLED HER HAIR away from her ear and listened harder as she lay in bed alongside Robbie. The chilly December gale shook the four corners of the lighthouse cottage and howled with an unmistakable sound. What she heard was not just the wind. It was a cry. A distinct ethereal cry that conjured childhood tales from Mo about the Bean Sidhe—ghostly women of the hills whose wail foretold death.

Meg tried to ignore this midnight disturbance. Her superstitious Irish Catholic mother would've already crossed herself three times and said a prayer of protection to the Blessed Virgin Mother. But Meg refused to believe such silliness.

She glanced over at Robbie, questioning how he could sleep through such screams—especially after she poked him a few times.

A shrilling howl shook the walls so fiercely it threatened to rip off the roof.

Meg kicked Robbie.

"Ugh," he woke. "Why'd you do that?"

"Listen."

The howling wind shuddered the window panes.

"Strong wind," Robbie mumbled on his pillow.

"The Bean Sidhe."

"What?" Robbie was half asleep.

"Irish banshees," Meg masked her nerves. "My mother always claimed the Bean Sidhe's howls foretold death."

"That's nice," Robbie rolled back to sleep.

"She swore she heard them the week my father died. She used to cross herself three times, say three *Hail Mary*'s, three *Our Father*'s, and three *Glory Be*'s."

"So do that and go back to sleep," Robbie mumbled on his pillow.

Meg scoffed at the notion.

The banshees screamed louder, and Meg's eyes widened nervously. The old lighthouse cottage creaked with ghosts.

Meg saw Robbie already asleep and swiftly crossed herself and snuck in a silent prayer.

"Better say a couple," Robbie grinned, his eyes still closed. "That storm's gonna blow all night."

Meg slapped him playfully—the sneak—and he chuckled, all the while the Bean Sidhe cried for death.

The days following the Bean Sidhe, Meg felt uneasy as snow and ice settled across the northern peninsula for a long winter, while the locals counted the days until the Door's only other season: July. Sure, a few tourists braved winter's cold and snow for a romantic bed & breakfast weekend in small-town seclusion. And on New Year's Day, Door County's Polar Bear Club conducted their annual swim in the frozen lake. But beyond the local pubs (at least three in each village), Door County remained a ghost town from Halloween to Memorial Day. Each village's hundred or so year-round residents cloistered themselves indoors, while rampant cabin fever prompted many to make weekly visits to Doc Johansen and profess their latest contrived ailment—all cured with a placebo, whiskey, or Playboy.

A small Hooverville of homemade ice-fishing shanties and parked vehicles appeared over the frozen lake a few hundred yards offshore. Smoke streamed from their steel pipe chimneys.

Robbie taught Meg the art of ice fishing (which pretty much involved warm clothes, booze, a lot of patience, and rarely fish). They cross-country skied under starlight. Skated upon the small stretch of frozen lake near Lighthouse Island.

Meg and Robbie picked up exactly where they left off. Meg spent the day tending to her postal duties and the shop, while Robbie embarked on Viking Season and oversaw operations at his fishery. In the evenings, they rendezvoused back at Lighthouse Island, where they ate dinner by candlelight, laughed and talked and made love until the wee hours. They gave themselves completely to each other, and as they lay naked in the other's arms, they longed to stay in the serenity of the moment forever.

"I love you," they whispered, saying the words without fear.

It felt like they had always been together. Everything seemed more vibrant, more purposeful, more alive now.

Meg found herself embracing the Irish shop. She created her own line of clothing. Entertained customers with an Irish brogue. Rediscovered her own childhood love for all things Irish. And even petitioned the City of Whitefish Creek for a permit to hold Door County's first-ever St. Patrick's Day Parade that coming March.

Robbie loved this side of her. "Say something Irish," he'd say in a mischievously aroused tone, as if asking her to talk dirty.

"I will in me brown."

"Ooo," he purred. "Say something else."

"Bag o' Schwag."

"Sexy."

"Say something Wisconsiny," Meg purred back.

"Dat's a right good bubbler, ay," Robbie's raised brow awaited Meg's purr...

"Yeah, that doesn't do it for me."

Mo called every day to ask about the shop and relay updates about Caitlyn.

"I don't trust that Irene," Mo began voicing her displeasure about the nanny. "She's deliberately keepin' the girls from her." She complained about Nick's work ethic, suspecting he was smoking pot again, and somewhere in the conversation, made sure to voice her displeasure about Meg's budding relationship with Robbie.

"Yer fallin' too fast," Mo accused Meg. "Yer mistakin' 'fallin' in luv' with real luv."

"I'm fine, mother."

"Yer horny," Mo said. "Anyone with a pulse and an ounce of libido can fall in luv. It requires no thought at all."

"Do you know how crazy you sound right now?" Meg disregarded her better judgment to hang up.

"Fallin' in luv is not 'real luv.' That's the prince on his steed sweepin' you off to his castle for happily ever after. Ha! Fairytales always end. Mark my words. It might take years, but at some point, you will be tested. Look at yer sister. Real honest-to-goodness luv is choosin' to luv someone even when you feel like breakin' their snot locker. That's real luv. That's when you grow. The other stuff is brainless bliss — "

" — I get it, mother — "

" — You'll get it when you get it. And I assure you, until yer tested, you don't get it. But it will come. As sure as the Claddagh. Then you'll discover if 'tis real luv or not."

"Do you think about the gloom and doom that comes out your mouth, or do you just open up and it spews out?"

The Fitzgibbons' Christmas card arrived the second week of December, which featured the four jailbirds with an unflattering image of Mo, nostrils flaring, eyes bugged, staring viciously at the camera with a naked Booker Wade grinning in the next cell.

"Look at me boat," a mortified Mo phoned Meg, dreading the hundreds of St. Louis friends who would be receiving this in the mail. "I look facially challenged!"

The Fitzgibbons' Christmas card always offered a fresh breath of real life from the scads of picture-perfect families posed on a beach in their white shirts and khakis. It started over three decades earlier when the Fitzgibbons' three-year-old triplets were at their peak of awful. And rather than perpetuate another bogus Christmas façade of three "perfect little angels," a nerve-shot Mary Lou sent a photo taken on the docks of Door County, with a worn George holding a fish, the three boys dirty, uncombed, one picking his nose, another crying, the third pulling the crying brother's hair, and an exhausted Mary Lou in grubby fishing clothes, hair a mess, no makeup, one jean leg rolled up to her knee, looking like she could scare rats from a barn.

People still laughed about it. In fact, the picture became such a piece of family history that Mary Lou blew it up and hung it over the fireplace mantle in their Door County home. Ever since, the Fitzgibbons' Christmas card featured just a real moment, usually something embarrassing, and was the card everyone looked forward to receiving each year.

"Tis the season to drink straight from the bottle," Mary Lou always said.

"Bleedin' weapon," Mo shook her head at her dear friend's twisted humor. "Have you got the holly bush yet?"

Like her pat-o'-lanterns, Mo shunned the American custom of Christmas trees, opting for the old Irish tradition of a holly bush. The abundance of holly bushes in Ireland allowed poor people to decorate their homes in the same way as those better off. And finding a holly bush with lots of berries brought especially good luck for the New Year. So Meg instituted "Operation Holly Bush." And one evening, under the cover of night, Robbie and she dressed in camouflage and face paint, drove down to Sturgeon Bay's country club and cut down a beautiful full-berried holly bush, laughing the whole way back. Growing up, Meg hated being the only kid on the block with a bush in their living room instead of a beautiful fir tree covered with ornaments. But as they placed the bush in the shop's bay window, she appreciated its simplicity and beauty, and the touch of Irish seasonal cheer it breathed into the shop.

Mo's relocation to Boston and Caitlyn's debilitating condition made it impractical to hold their big McKenna family Christmas gathering, so all the siblings remained in their respectable cities, calling Boston to wish Mo and their beloved sister a "Merry Christmas."

Meg poured a glass of wine and called Caitlyn, Mo, and Mary Lou on speaker phone to reinstitute their traditional Christmas Eve rip session of the season's deluge of brag letters disguised as holiday cheer. As usual, their sister-in-law Chelsea took top prize, boasting how "blessed" they were, and "Praise God," "God is good," "Let God into your lives," how their two children had straight A's, how their 5th grader was selected to play Jesus in the school play, how Chelsea is training for the San Francisco marathon, and how they just bought a $800,000 home—and got it for $650,000!

"You know what you tell her," Mary Lou said. "Tell her you just Googled her house, it's lovely, and they should know, the local police website lists two known sex offenders living in their neighborhood."

They laughed hard, Caitlyn especially.

After ending the call with "I love you," Meg prepared Mo's usual Christmas Eve dinner of cranberry sauce, potatoes, stuffing, carrots, and a Christmas goose (none of which turned out as picture perfect as Mo's). The Christmas goose she cooked too long. The potatoes she didn't cook long enough. The cranberry sauce looked more like a bad jello mold. And Robbie ate it all, heaping praise on Meg's culinary foray, taking seconds and thirds. And even though Meg suspected it was just to make her feel better, she appreciated it all the same.

For dessert, she baked a loaf of her mother's delicious soda bread, filled with caraway seeds and raisins, which turned out perfect. She lit a large glowing candle in the middle of the kitchen table, set out Mo's fine china, placed the bread and a pitcher of milk alongside, and keeping with Irish tradition, unlatched the front door so that the Blessed Virgin Mary and St. Joseph, or any wandering traveler (St. Nicholas perhaps), could step out of the cold and partake in their Irish hospitality.

They exchanged gifts before the roaring fire.

Meg gave Robbie the framed mug shot of herself, and an Aran fisherman's sweater she knitted.

Robbie surprised her by converting the upstairs light tower into a small sketch studio, with art supplies and an easel. And knowing his fear of heights made it all the more special.

The next morning, Meg faced one of her phobias, instructing Robbie to drive them north to Sister Bay's small Catholic chapel for Christmas mass to pray for her sister, hoping her long absence from church wouldn't subject them to a lightning bolt the moment they crossed its threshold.

"We're just here for the wine, thanks," Meg joked as she smiled at an usher, taking a back-row seat with Robbie.

"Isn't that sacrilegious?" Robbie shifted uncomfortably, having sworn off church two decades earlier when his father died.

Meg whispered back: "Jesus's first miracle was turning water into wine. If that's not a green light to start drinking, I don't know what is."

They both chuckled, easing their apprehensions, and Meg reached out for Robbie's hand appreciatively, knowing this was not easy for him either.

As Meg knelt in the peacefulness of the small church, taking in the Christmas surroundings that included the hand-carved wooden manger at the foot of the alter, the surrounding poinsettias, a simple Christmas tree in one corner, and the light organ rendition of *Hark the Herald Angels Sing*, she flashed back to Christmas mornings as a child, with Mo dragging them all to mass and Meg protesting.

Caitlyn always eased Meg's apprehension by holding her hand during prayer, and now Meg felt that same soothing strength in Robbie's. She squeezed him tight, wanting to hold onto this moment forever. A moment when everything seemed right. Anything seemed possible. A moment that would scare the bejaysus out of her superstitious mother's abiding sense of tragedy.

Mo's Good Day Bad Day Theory held when things seemed this perfect, something ghastly loomed just around the corner. It's what gave life balance. Nothing remained idyllic. Not according to Irishmen. Life was about perseverance and hardship. Finding inner strength and character through adversity. That's how we achieved personal growth in our short time on earth, Mo preached. Not lying in the sun eating bonbons.

Meg held Robbie's hand firmly as they departed the chapel, hoping moments like these could last forever.

A cold, wicked wind blew fierce off the lake with a wail Meg recognized.

All the exiting church participants stopped in their tracks, noting the foreboding howl and pulling tight their coats to protect themselves from the chilly assault.

The Bean Sidhe.

Meg squeezed Robbie's hand to the point it cut off his circulation.

"Ouch," Robbie chuckled.

Meg did not laugh. Nor relax her grip. The louder and fiercer the Bean Sidhe howled, the tighter she squeezed.

"Easy," Robbie laughed. "I'm not going anywhere. Let's hurry, before that wind blows us away," he picked up his pace, holding her hand as they rushed to the truck.

Meg forced a smile, chiding herself for succumbing to Mo's crazy superstition. But she could not relax. The wail of the Bean Sidhe echoed its death call.

CHAPTER 34

LITTLE CHRISTMAS

"Beer makes you feel the way you ought to feel without beer."

—*Irishman Henry Lawson*

CAITLYN'S 5'2" FRAME WASTED to all of 90 pounds when she completed her chemo and radiation. She felt tired and weak, and without a stomach to store food, her daily diet consisted of six small meals, with a generous regimen of high-calorie power bars to maintain weight. Her scans showed no signs of metastasis, which even the most skeptical doctors found encouraging given the aggressive nature of the cancer. And with all her paid leave exhausted and Nick's part-time medical equipment sales sporadic at best, she returned to work to produce some desperately needed income, while Irene remained in the house as full-time nanny and housekeeper, leaving Mo the third wheel.

"I'll be back for Little Christmas," Mo telephoned Meg, the exhaustion in her voice evident. "Mary Lou is flyin' up. We're both gettin' into Green Bay around noon. Just make sure you take down the Christmas decorations that mornin' before you pick us up," Mo said. "We can all go out afterwards and get a little iron in our blood." That was code word for "drink heavily." "And don't take them down the day before," Mo cautioned. "Do it first thing in the mornin'."

Mo kept the steadfast Irish tradition of taking down Christmas decorations January 6th, the Feast of the Epiphany. She swore it was bad luck to do so anytime before or after.

January 6th also marked the old Irish custom of Little Christmas, more formally known as Little Women's Christmas. It harkened back to days of big Irish families, when all household duties fell on women, and men never lifted a finger, except this one day, when all men in Ireland granted their tired wives, exhausted from the holidays, a day to relax without guilt. It was also the one day of the year respectable women could enter the pubs without shame to enjoy pints of stout with friends until the wee hours.

Mary Lou swore Mo turned into another woman on Little Christmas. An alter ego she dubbed "Lola" emerged. The two best friends would leave the house around dinner time, dressed to the nines, and Meg and Caitlyn would hear stories the next day from Mary Lou about their mother dancing and drinking into the wee hours, and after a good fill of Guinness, turning into a full-fledged klepto, stealing empty bar glasses, pitchers, and trinkets everywhere they went. And if they happened across a live band with a tambourine—which Mo always sniffed out—she climbed on stage, seized the instrument, and started swatting "arses" in the crowd.

"This is HUGE," Meg told Robbie, explaining the mythical accounts of "Lola" and Little Christmas. "They've never asked any kids along. It's like they're initiating me," she exclaimed giddily. "I finally get to see Lola! Wait. How am I going to get everything done? Take down the Christmas decorations. Deliver the mail. Pick them up in Green Bay by noon..."

"We can do the decorations now," Robbie said.

"It's bad luck! They have to be taken down on Little Christmas morning."

"She's not going to know."

"She'll know. She has this weird ESP. No matter how good I lie, she always knows."

"Well, I dropped some nets out by Washington Island that I have to pull up tomorrow," Robbie said. "They say there's another big ice storm movin' in. But other than that, I can deliver the mail."

"You'd do that?" Meg beamed. "But you're not an authorized mail carrier. That's a federal offense."

"Nobody 'round here cares."

"I can lose my job."

"One time's not gonna matter. Look, I know everyone. I know where they live. You shouldn't be drivin' that car of yours in this snow anyway. Not without a plow. Let me do it. Then you can get initiated into your Little Christmas thing. You'll have to leave early anyways for the airport to beat the storm."

Meg mulled over his generous proposal.

"Look, you can swear me in," Robbie said. "I'll even put that mail carrier license plate on my truck. Then I'm official."

"Can I do that?"

"You're Whitefish Creek's Post Master," Robbie shrugged.

The two spent the night on Light House Island. Meg awoke late to discover Robbie had already departed. She showered, then stepped into the winter wonderland to find new snow tires on her car. A note on her driver's seat read: *Drive safe.*

She smiled at the sweet gesture, wishing Robbie was still around to make love to.

Meg drove across the frozen stretch of ice from Lighthouse Island to the mainland with much better traction than when she arrived. Ice covered the lake for three to four miles out. A few people even reported a solid path from Whitefish Creek all the way to Chambers Island (about 7 miles out).

Meg spent the morning taking down the shop's Christmas decorations and lights. By nine o'clock, she completed the task by dragging their dry, ill-gotten holly bush outside for trash pickup. Cold gray consumed the sky. Flurries filled the air. Below-freezing temperatures bit into exposed flesh, and Meg could just hear Mary Lou: "Good Gawd! It's cold enough to freeze the balls off a brass monkey."

Meg hurried towards the shop. The same wicked wind from Christmas screamed off the frozen lake like a hundred Bean Sidhes, prickling the back of her neck, as the howls seemed particularly desperate. Her insides sickened with a fear for those closest to her. Caitlyn. Robbie. Her mother and Mary Lou flying on a plane.

Meg gazed over the bay of ice. About a mile offshore, a stream of smoke rose from the farthest ice fishing shanty. And somewhere out in the gray void Robbie checked his nets.

She wanted to call him to ease her paranoia, but you couldn't get a cell phone signal on the lake. Not that Robbie ever used his cell phone anyway. Anna had given it to him years before and most of the time it just sat home collecting dust because he hated being that accessible, and he never checked his messages.

Damn Bean Sidhes! Meg fumed for allowing Mo's ridiculous superstitions to play with her head.

By the time Meg crossed the drawbridge into Sturgeon Bay, snow fell in big marshmallow flakes. The 90-minute drive to Green Bay's airport took over two hours. And her head began to play games. Something felt wrong.

She called Caitlyn to ease any fears the cancer had returned and to ensure Mo's plane departed okay.

She called Mary Lou, who sat stranded in the St. Louis airport waiting for a delayed flight.

She tried Robbie's cell phone. No answer as expected. She tried Robbie's home phone, the winery, and finally reached Donnie Kodanko, the assistant winemaker who assumed Anna's position.

"Haven't seen him since yesterday," Donnie reported. "I thought he said he was gonna pull his nets before that storm hit, ay. Did you try the processing plant?"

"No answer," Meg said.

"I reckon Judd's with him," Donnie noted about the fish processing plant's foreman.

A foreboding feeling gnawed at Meg all the way to Green Bay.

Mo's flight landed just before they shut down the airport, and Mary Lou called from St. Louis to insist they start Little Christmas without her.

During the three-hour drive to Door County, Mo discussed her worries about Caitlyn.

Mo reported how Nick brought in some slick lawyer who kept pushing Caitlyn to sign papers to authorize a malpractice suit against her primary care doctor, and Caitlyn kept pushing him off. She didn't want to sue anyone. She just wanted to get better.

"That Irene lets the girls do whatever they want," Mo disapproved. "So does Nick's mother. They're goin' to turn them into brats. And we have to play the bad cop."

Megan was also demanding Caitlyn stop the chemo treatments, unsettled by Caitlyn's deteriorating appearance. "You're always taking medicine," Mo quoted Megan. "It makes you lose your hair!" Then Caitlyn smiled at her confused daughter and assured her the medicine was helping. "No it's not! It's making you too sick to play with us," Mo again quoted Megan, "Irene's never sick!"

Mo said that Caitlyn just smiled softly at her oldest daughter with the patience of Job. She knew her condition frightened Megan, who was just trying to process all these emotions that no child of five should ever deal with.

It broke Meg's heart to hear all this. Caitlyn deserved so much better.

They arrived back in Whitefish Creek after 6 p.m.

The falling snow whipped the northern peninsula into a

white blur, and still no word from Robbie.

Meg dropped Mo off at the shop to freshen up for their evening, and drove down Main Street through a foot of freshly fallen snow.

When she unlocked the post office door and entered the back room, she discovered the day's return mail absent.

Her stomach knotted.

Robbie never made it back to the post office.

CHAPTER 35

DEATH'S DOOR

*May you be in heaven a half hour before
the devil knows you're dead.*

—Irish saying

SHERIFF BALDY BRIDENHAGEN ORGANIZED a search party in one of the worst whiteouts of memory. They alerted the Coast Guard and headed onto the frozen passage of Death's Door (the treacherous waterway between Lake Michigan and Green Bay where many ships met their watery graves). A nearly seven-mile-wide expanse of ice covered the deadly passage, connecting the peninsula's northernmost tip to Washington Island.

They ventured out with ropes and spotlights and bullhorns. Over a hundred people fanned out over the frozen lake on four wheelers, snowmobiles, and pickup trucks. The fierce snow restricted visibility to about ten feet from their faces as spirits of drowned sailors howled in the wind.

An ice fisherman off Whitefish Creek, Hans Knuppel,

reported seeing Robbie and Judd Weborg driving across the ice towards Chambers Island just before the bulk of the storm hit about four hours earlier. They stopped to see how the fish were biting, and said they were pulling up nets before the storm hit. Hans recalled them mentioning something about nets off Washington Island.

The search party spanned from Whitefish Creek to Washington Island. They set up a command center at Al Johnson's Swedish Restaurant, midway between the two points.

Meg snowmobiled into the whiteout with Baldy Bridenhagen, relying on its GPS to guide them across the ice to Alewife Alma's place. The blinding snow diluted Plum Island's range lights into a ghostly beam, barely visible outside of a mile. When they reached her snow-covered house, they found her wearing the dress Meg gave her.

"Alma," Meg called, "Have you seen Robbie today? He was out checking his nets this afternoon right as the worst of the storm hit," Meg said desperately. "He's missing. Do you have any idea where he could be?"

Alma thought. "There's a favorite fishing hole of his about a mile due west of here."

They piled onto the snowmobile with Alma pointing the way.

A half-hour later, Walter Gunnlaugsson and Jack Newgaard, both fellow fishermen, combed another favorite fishing spot about two miles west of Plum Island and reported broken ice 2 ½ miles north of Gill's Rock.

"Looks like something went through," they radioed Baldy.

Meg gasped.

"Give me your coordinates," Baldy asked, punching them into his GPS, then radioed them to the Coast Guard.

Meg didn't breathe from the moment she heard "something went through" to the time they arrived at the scene.

The news numbed her body to the point she no longer felt the biting cold or sting of flurries needling her face as they sped through the whiteout.

When they reached the broken ice, the Coast Guard already diverted their search efforts to investigate the break. The hole loomed about fifteen feet away. Broken sheets of ice floated in the dark void. The serrated edges surrounding the hole looked about eight inches thick. The opening itself was about a 20-foot radius. Big enough for Robbie's truck to fall through.

Meg's stomach twisted sick.

"Find anything?" Baldy asked the Coast Guard.

"Maybe some tire tracks over there," the man pointed to a spot north of the hole. "Hard to tell. Snow covered everything."

"Lake's probably fifty feet deep here," Baldy noted. "Freezing temperatures."

Baldy glanced around the whiteout, discerning the conditions. "If anyone made it out in this storm, they wouldn't've known which way was the mainland."

"Not without a compass," the Coast Guardsman noted.

They called in the entire search party and fanned everyone in all directions.

About a mile further north, 3 ½ miles off Gill's Rock,

the Coast Guard stumbled across a four-foot oval hole cut into a foot of ice, with a six-foot pole protruding from the surface and a small red flag attached to the top.

"No nets," they reported. "They probably pulled them up and were on their way back."

They searched all through the night.

Water temperatures proved colder than anticipated, limiting dive times. And the notoriously strong currents of Death's Door made it a struggle.

They located The Northern Lights Fishing Company truck at the bottom of the dark lake not far from the open hole.

License plate issue: *Mail U.S. Postal Carrier.*

When Meg explained the circumstances behind her Postal Carrier license plate, a collective gasp resounded amongst the locals. The mail carrier's curse!

Meg confirmed Robbie's swearing in as a postal carrier. And everyone gasped again, as if Meg willed this death sentence upon their beloved fisherman.

Coast Guard divers affirmed the pitch-black conditions, freezing temperatures, and difficult currents. Even if Robbie and Judd escaped the truck, they had thirty seconds before their muscles froze and they sank.

Harsh conditions halted operations soon after, but not before divers found Judd Weborg's body a hundred meters from the site. Recovery of Robbie's body needed to wait.

CHAPTER 36

IRISH WAKE

The sleep that knows no wake, is followed by the wake that knows no sleep.

—Irish saying

IT SEEMED LIKE THE ENTIRE PENINSULA drifted into Al Johnson's like a bunch of zombies numb with disbelief. This couldn't happen. Not to the Supreme Lutefisk. Not to their master fish boiler, parade float driver, Fourth of July pyrotechnician, Door County's beloved fisherman and most eligible bachelor.

No more would his unmistakable Northern Lights Fishing Company truck rattle around the Door.

Children's hearts broke all over the peninsula. They lost their hero. Their Davy Crocket, their Captain Kirk, their Robin Hood, Babe Ruth. He treated all the children like his equal. Taught them about responsibility and hard work. Helped them build forts and tree houses, and led them on countless adventures on the high seas.

Mo reached a supportive hand across the wood table

and squeezed Meg's tight.

"I heard the Bean Sidhe," Meg whispered morosely. "I shouldn't've let him deliver the mail. It's my fault."

"That's ballsch," Mo dismissed the notion.

"If he wasn't hurrying back to deliver it, he would've been more cautious," Meg beat herself up.

"You don't know that," Mo insisted. "You have to trust there's a higher plan. You must. That's what got me through your father."

"When my Bill died," a woman at the bar spoke. "Timmy was nine and Jimmy was seven...I never thought we'd recover. Robbie took Tim and Jimmy under his wing. Gave them jobs on his boat. Then his processing plant. Taught them how to be outstanding young men..." she trailed off with tears.

"He never asked anything from anybody," another man noted.

"He could never say 'no' to anyone who needed help," a woman said.

Everyone agreed.

"Remember those screwy 'wake-up calls,'" a man chuckled.

All in-the-know laughed.

"Every morning. He'd come down to the docks, get his boat ready to ship out, then he'd run back home for that stupid morning wake-up call from Alewife Alma. Remember that? I told him, why bother? You're up. And he said if he wasn't there to answer, Alma wouldn't feel useful. So I said why don't you have her call earlier? And he said he wanted her to sleep in. He did that for years, remember?"

They all chuckled.

"He could eat some serious lutefisk," Chairman Philpot admired.

Meg laughed. Others raised their glasses in the Supreme Lutefisk's honor.

"I don't think I knew anyone who owned ten of the same flannel shirts," Doc Sugarbaker commented.

More chuckles.

"Do you remember his batter-fried smelt recipe?"

"That was awful," people laughed.

People recalled funny stories about Robbie and Judd. And Meg enjoyed the levity. It felt like an Irish wake.

An elder dental hygienist recounted how the moment Robbie discovered they shared the same birth date, he called every year without fail to wish her a happy birthday.

Then there was Robbie's old fishing mentor, Selwyn Picker, who said Robbie stopped by every day on his delivery route just to say "hey dare" and see if he needed anything.

They reminisced about Robbie's baseball prowess as a boy, many proclaiming him the best baseball player the upper peninsula ever produced. His ability to drive a baseball 400 feet by age 13 placed him on a god-like pedestal that Robbie refused to claim. Even today, stories still echoed from the pubs about his astonishing feats on the diamond. Accolades Robbie cared nothing for. By 16, he dropped out of high school altogether to become a full-time fisherman, never looking back or succumbing to the vast local pressure to continue his athletic legacy, and never spoke of it again. Something Meg never knew, which impressed her all the more.

Everyone had a story about Robbie.

Drinks flowed. Humorous anecdotes abounded, reminiscing about their beloved fisherman. The shared laughter offered a temporary escape from the pain of loss. And the more they hurt, the more they wanted to laugh.

More and more villagers arrived at Al Johnson's as news spread. Not even the winter storm kept them away. When their resident hermit, Alewife Alma, walked through Al's big oak doors, the room silenced. The rare sighting was like seeing a fish walk on land. She stood in the doorway wearing her homemade beaver coat. Her dark eyes surveyed the room. Then Door County's recluse marched over to the McKennas and sat at their table.

"My ma had one of those," Alma pointed to Mo's rosary, then reached into her fur coat. Meg saw her dress underneath as Alma pulled out a bottle of homemade moonshine. "Snort?" she offered a flask, and both Meg and Mo happily accepted.

Everyone wanted to endure this tragedy together, sharing stories, and drinking, and experiencing laughter through tears. The tales even moved Mo, as she sat alongside her broken daughter in a show of support.

For a man who wasn't religious, Mo commented, Robbie seemed to live a life more Christian than most Christians she knew.

By ten o'clock, laughter and camaraderie filled the Swedish Restaurant. They toasted Robbie for the example he set, then a wave of screams and gasps erupted.

The ghostly figure appeared in the gathering's midst.

The phantom stood like winter itself. A ghastly mummy

of snow and ice. Its face black. Dressed in Meg's Irish sweater.

Robbie's ghost!

Meg's heart stopped.

People screamed.

Then the figure collapsed.

Doc Sugarbaker and others like Meg rushed to him. His body felt ice cold. Frostbite ate his face and hands. Snow and ice mummified him. But it was Robbie.

"Robbie," Meg shouted repeatedly in his ear.

"Call an ambulance," Doc Sugarbaker shouted, hunched over Robbie. "His pupils aren't responding." Robbie's dilated pupils failed to respond to light. Doc gripped his wrist. "I can't get a pulse. Get me a jacket and put it under his neck."

"Robbie," Meg demanded. "It's me! Open your eyes."

"Get his clothes off, they're soaked," Doc commanded. "Get some blankets."

Meg and others cut off Robbie's frozen clothes as Doc furiously administered CPR.

The ambulance arrived five minutes later. Two paramedics rushed in. "Do you have a pulse?"

"No," Doc Sugarbaker conceded. "I couldn't get one. He's ice cold."

The paramedics gently log-rolled Robbie onto a backboard, placed his head and neck in a C-collar, and continued CPR as they carted him to the ambulance.

"Let me go with him," Meg followed them to the ambulance. "Please."

"Are you family?" the paramedic asked.

Meg hesitated. "No, but...."

"Sorry," he hopped aboard.

Doc climbed into the back of the ambulance. "I'll look after him," he reassured Meg.

The paramedic prepared the defibrillators as the doors shut, and Meg watched the ambulance rush off in a blare of sirens.

"Hurry, we'll follow them," Mo grabbed Meg by the arm and raced her to their old Cadillac.

Meg and Mo pursued the ambulance to Sturgeon Bay and Door County's Memorial hospital. They cut the normal 45-minute drive to 30 minutes. To Meg's surprise, Mo drove pedal to the floor in snowy conditions, breaching 90 mph at one point from a woman known to never exceed 60. Even Meg felt the danger of their speed in snowy conditions.

"Say a rosary," Mo motioned to the glove compartment. Meg popped it open and found the wooden strand of Celtic beads with the attached cross of St. Brigid.

"I believe in God, the Father Almighty..." Mo prayed the Apostles Creed.

Even though Meg hadn't recited the words in over fourteen years, the prayer remained hardwired into her brain from years of Catholic school imprisonment, and she joined in, finding it a proactive diversion from the stress of whether Robbie reached the hospital alive.

The ambulance arrived five minutes ahead of them.

Mo dropped Meg off at the ER to the roaring sound of a helicopter lifting off the pad.

"I'm looking for Robbie Knudson," Meg rushed to the front desk. "The ambulance just brought him here."

The woman knew without punching into the computer.

"They're transporting him to Froedtert Memorial in Milwaukee."

"That helicopter taking off?"

"Yes," the woman confirmed. "It's one of Wisconsin's two Trauma One Centers."

"So he's alive?" Meg clutched hope.

"Yes. Critical, but yes. He's alive."

Meg felt herself breathe for the first time in 30 minutes. She hurried to the sliding glass entrance doors where she ran into Mo, Chairman Philpot, and several others.

"He's alive," Meg rejoiced. "They're taking him to Milwaukee."

"Praise be to Jaysus," Mo gasped.

"He's critical. But he's alive," Meg stepped into the cold to watch the southbound helicopter disappear into the night.

"Doc!" Chairman Philpot spotted Dr. Sugarbaker walking towards them from inside the ER. The sliding glass doors opened.

"How is he?" Meg asked.

Doc shook his head, still in disbelief. "You hear things like this…"

"What?" everyone pressed.

"He flat lined. His body temp was seventy degrees. We tried to get a heartbeat for damn near twenty minutes. I hit him with that defibrillator over a dozen times and nothing. He was DOA. He was DOA two minutes from the ER and his heart started beating. I've never seen anything like it."

"I'll get the car," Mo said.

The two of them said two rosaries on the three-hour

drive to Milwaukee. The second one at Meg's request.

CHAPTER 37

IRISH VIGIL

The grace of God is found between the saddle and the ground.

—Irish saying

IT WASN'T A QUESTION of whether or not Robbie suffered brain damage, but how much, the doctors said. And that's if he survived. He remained comatose. His vitals critical. Amputation of both feet, his hands and nose seemed inevitable.

Robbie lay hooked to all kinds of monitors. Bandages covered his face, hands, and feet, with his protruding toes and fingers coal black from frostbite. I.V. fluids bloated him to the point he looked a hundred pounds heavier as he clung to life.

"You need to go home and get some rest," Mo told Meg. She had not slept in three days.

"I'm staying."

"There's nothin' you can do," Mo insisted. "Come back to Door County, take a shower, eat, rest, then come back."

"Would you do that with Caitlyn?" Meg said.

Mo eyed Meg's resolve. "Here," she walked over to the nurse desk and asked for a pen and paper, then scribbled a few sentences. "Take this. Say it nine times every day for nine days at nine o'clock every mornin'."

"What is this?"

"The novena to St. Jude. Patron Saint of Desperate Cases. I'll be sayin' it at the same time for Robbie. Remember, nine times, nine o'clock, every mornin'. Startin' tomorrow. Don't forget."

Meg smiled. "I thought you didn't like Robbie."

Mo smiled. "I thought you didn't like me shop."

Meg nodded, touché.

They did not hug. That was not their nature. Nor did the words "I love you" escape from their lips. But they held each other's gaze for an endearing moment, and for the first time in decades, they felt a shared bond.

"Nine times at nine. Don't forget. And the moment he wakes up, write the word 'Jaysus' on a strip of paper and put it in his food."

Meg smiled: classic Mo.

Caitlyn called to check in on Robbie's status. "I called my prayer chain out here. I think they're excited to pray for someone other than me for a change."

"Thanks," Meg chuckled. And it surprised a skeptic like Meg to find so much comfort in this.

By mid-morning, Robbie's brothers began arriving. Meg introduced herself to each, who were polite, but like Robbie's mother years earlier, regarded her as nothing more than transient. But when Anna stepped into the waiting room later that day, having flown in from California,

Robbie's brothers lit up. She was a trusted friend. Everyone from Door County swarmed her like the returning homecoming queen, looking to her to spearhead Robbie's care. After all, she was one of their own. And Meg, no matter how long she lived in Door County, was forever a FISH, and now felt invisible.

Meg spent another night in the hospital, this time making small talk with Anna, who now headed winemaking operations at a large vineyard in Sonoma County, while Riley took music classes at Berkeley at age 17.

"You look great," Meg said sincerely.

"So do you," Anna smiled. A total lie. Meg hadn't showered or changed clothes in five days, and she knew her grubby appearance frightened small children.

"I'll be here all night. Go home and get some rest," Anna offered sweetly.

Not a chance, Meg thought.

Two weeks passed and Robbie remained comatose. His vitals held, but the gangrene in his extremities reached a critical point that required amputation. Meg studied everything about gangrene and amputations on the Internet and fought to buy a few more days for Robbie.

"It won't change anything," the doctors reassured them. "The longer we wait, the higher risk of infection to other parts of his body."

Meg pushed Robbie's brothers, who held legal authority to decide, and they finally conceded to delay a few days.

"If I see any indication that poisons entered the rest of his blood stream, I'm amputating," the doctor conceded.

Meg decided to throw up a Hail Mary, literally, and

called Mo.

Mo called in an order of charismatic nuns outside Milwaukee. They all showed up Saturday morning at the hospital and formed a prayer circle outside the ICU, all linking hands, along with Meg, who didn't squirm at the holy show of it all. Meg said more prayers that day than she had her entire life, and for the first time, actually felt them.

Come Monday, the doctors took pause at some unexpected improvement in Robbie's hands. His right hand in particular. On second look, it appeared more a dark yellowy brown than the black, leathery feel of normal gangrene. A curious development that prompted the doctors to delay a course of action a few more days. But his nose needed amputation. Same with his feet. The doctors recommended amputating his entire lower leg below the knee, which statistically produced far better results than the alternative midfoot amputation, and worked better with current prosthetics.

"We'll have them design a new prosthetic," Meg pleaded, showing them her medical research on successful midfoot amputations. "Don't cut his legs if there's another way," she begged the surgeon before he amputated.

"No promises," the surgeon said, then surprised himself with his innovative technique in adding more foot padding, and managed to pull off a midfoot amputation, at least for the time being.

"Thank you," Meg hugged him.

"He's lucky to have you," the surgeon smiled.

At some point in the middle of the night, Meg awoke and saw Anna sleeping on the couch across from her. The clock on the wall read a quarter after three. Meg felt hungry for the first time in weeks. She passed the nurse's desk on the way to the cafeteria and paused.

"Nothing new," the brunette nurse smiled.

"Thanks, Kim," Meg knew the staff by name.

She took the elevator down to the cafeteria and found a vending machine with some granola bars, then visited the bathroom and washed her face. When she returned upstairs, Kim was no longer at the nurses' desk and Anna no longer on the couch.

Maybe she went to the bathroom, Meg surmised, settling back into her lounger. After twenty minutes ticked by and no Anna, Meg walked back to check with Kim.

"There you are," Kim smiled.

"I was over there," Meg pointed to the waiting room around the corner.

"We must've just missed each other. I went to find you in the cafeteria. He opened his eyes."

Meg's heart leapt.

"Your friend's back there now. Come on, I'll take you."

Kim escorted Meg towards the ICU.

"No more visitors," the ICU nurse stopped them. "We need to change his dressings."

"I need to see him," Meg pleaded. "Just for a second. Please. I've been waiting out here for weeks."

"Are you his wife?"

"No, but…."

"Sorry. You'll need to wait," the ICU nurse let Anna walk out then shut the unit's glass door.

Meg tried to glimpse Robbie through the ICU window,

anything to see him, but several machines and another patient blocked her view.

"He still has bandages all over his face," Anna said. "He's really weak. He couldn't talk, but he was happy to see someone he knew. I could tell."

Meg's stomach sickened. She should've been the first one Robbie saw when he awoke.

"I need to call Eddie, George, and Max," Anna was elated, reaching for her cell phone to dial Robbie's brothers.

Robbie slept the next twenty-four hours. His condition remained critical. His vitals exhibited some stabilization, but the question of brain damage loomed. Doctors continued to monitor his hands, and postponed a decision for another couple days.

The ICU's regulations limited visitors to three at a time. When Robbie opened his eyes again, it was mid-morning. Kim, the night nurse, already clocked out, and the day nurse rightfully admitted Robbie's three brothers for visitation. They remained with Robbie until the ICU nurse shooed them away like a protective mama bear, leaving Meg once again to wait.

Later that afternoon, a nurse presented a disheartened Meg a letter addressed to her, sent in care of the hospital with her sister's return address. Meg opened it. No note. No letter. Just an envelope full of beach sand. Meg smiled with her whole face and chuckled as she recalled the time she mailed sand in Caitlyn's time of need. It was the perfect thing to brighten an otherwise cloudy day.

Meg loved her sister dearly.

That night, Kim discretely walked over and whispered to

Meg, noting Anna asleep on the adjacent couch. "He's awake."

Meg's heart leapt. She quickly stood to follow.

"Is he awake?" Anna's groggy voice called.

"I didn't want to wake you," Kim said. "It's just a routine check. He's probably still out."

"I'll go," Anna stretched. "My neck's killing me. You guys really need to get better couches."

Kim's eyes apologized to Meg.

Thanks for trying, Meg's lips moved in silence.

The moment they saw Robbie's opened eyes in the ICU, Anna pushed through Meg and rushed to his side.

"You're up! How are you feeling? I'm so glad you got to see George, Max, and Eddie."

Robbie blinked. Bandages covered most of his face. Meg witnessed the flat surface where his amputated nose once protruded. His feet were wrapped in bandages and looked like giant fists with half his foot amputated. But his hands encouragingly looked more of a jaundiced brown than black, appearing soft to the touch, not leathery like gangrene.

Anna babbled on as Meg pulled up short of the ICU bed. She could not stop staring at Robbie's blue eyes, searching for any hint he was okay.

Robbie's gaze wandered off Anna as if sensing Meg's presence. And the moment their eyes met, Meg wanted to dive inside them, but Robbie's faded inward, turning away from Meg, as if wanting to distance himself.

"Are you okay?" Anna asked Robbie, flashing a scornful look at Meg.

Robbie raised his bandaged hand a few inches off the

bed, his eyes gritting in frustration at his inability to lift higher, and he slammed it down angrily.

"What's wrong?" Anna asked concerned.

A harsh rasp emoted from his mouth as he thrashed his head. His monitor started to beep. His heart rate quickened. The ICU nurse appeared in seconds.

"What happened?" the nurse demanded.

"I don't know," Anna said. "One second he was fine, then…"

The ICU nurse threw a look at Meg that could turn a person to stone.

"It's okay," the ICU nurse reassured Robbie. "Calm down, it's okay."

Robbie continued to pound on the bed with his bandaged hand, refusing to look back at Meg.

"Both of you leave," the ICU nurse demanded.

Meg hesitated, wanting to help Robbie.

"Leave!" the ICU nurse said.

Anna grabbed Meg's hand and pulled her out of the ICU unit as if she were a disobedient child. "What did you do?" Anna accused her outside.

"I don't know," Meg said, feeling her stomach tighten into a hard, sick knot.

Meg did not see Robbie the entire next day. Her mind replayed his unsettling reaction over and over again, as she sat in the waiting room, agonizing and blaming herself.

"Anna," nurse Kim walked into the waiting room. "He wants to see you."

"He spoke?" Meg beamed, standing from the couch.

"Yes," Kim offered a faint smile.

"How is he? Mentally? Is he okay?" Anna asked.

"We still don't know. We'll need to run tests. Follow me."

Meg waited for the same invitation to visit. "Can I see him?"

Kim sadly looked at Meg. "He just asked for Anna."

The words struck like a blow to the head.

"I'll give you a full report," Anna reassured Meg, which made her feel worse.

The next few days, Meg heard miraculous reports that Robbie defied statistics and showed no evidence of brain damage.

Robbie recounted falling through the ice, which Anna relayed to the group. Apparently, they were driving back from their last nets just as the bulk of the storm hit, trying a find a smoother route to the mainland, and the ice cracked beneath them. Judd was at the wheel. Robbie said the truck went down nose first and sank fast. Judd splashed into the freezing water in a panic. Robbie leapt from the passenger side. The lower half of his body plunged into what felt like a thousand stabbing knives. He called for Judd repeatedly. No answer. As hypothermia set in, a disoriented Robbie managed to pull himself out. He knew he needed to keep moving. The snow blinded his way to the mainland. He walked for miles through the blizzard, and ended up on one of the Sister Islands where he stumbled across a ramshackle, rotted shed and collapsed inside, better left for dead. Then something made him open his eyes. He didn't know when or where or how much time elapsed. His body felt numb. Snow covered him from the holes in the roof. He banged his frozen arms and feet to awaken some movement, pulled himself up, and walked until he saw the faint light of the Swedish Restaurant guiding him into Sister Bay. That was the last thing he remembered.

Everyone agreed it was a miracle he survived.

The doctors continued to push off a decision on his hands. They talked about scheduling a surgery to reconstruct his nose with tissue from his ear. And Meg continued her vigil in the waiting room, saying her morning novena, nine times, at nine o'clock. When she needed a smile, she peeked at the envelope of beach sand she carried in her pocket.

The next afternoon, Mo sat at Meg's side when Anna walked into the waiting room and announced that Robbie wanted to see Meg.

Meg's heart leapt. She stood, feeling her stomach knot as she walked to the ICU.

The absence of Robbie's facial bandages revealed a face with a flat scar of skin where his nose once protruded.

Meg smiled gently, trying not to show shock, nor wanting to cause another negative reaction. And when she gazed into his eyes, they seemed distant.

Robbie's voice sounded weak. "They said you haven't left the hospital."

"No."

Silence settled until Robbie finally spoke. "Go home."

The words cut. "Did I do something? I know your life has changed. But we'll get through this. We will — "

" — I'm the one who needs to get through this," he said coldly.

"I can help you — "

" — I don't want your help. Do you understand? I'm the one who has to live without feet or hands or a face. Look at me. You don't want this. I'm not the person you knew anymore. I'll never be that person again."

Meg shook her head, tears in her eyes, refusing to leave. "You're wrong."

"You're a distraction. There's no place for you anymore."

Meg could not believe her ears.

"Go home," Robbie rasped. "It's time to move on again. I need to do this myself."

Meg shook her head, hurt, but not backing away.

"It's not good for either of us if you stay," Robbie said.

Meg gritted a stalwart smile. "If you think you're doing me a favor pushing me away because you think I'd have a better life without you, you're an idiot! I don't care if you don't have feet, hands, nose, whatever. You want your space. Have it. But I'm not going anywhere. I'm staying in Door County. I'm delivering your mail. And I'm working in the Irish shop until I rot."

Meg marched out the ICU, and walked until she found a tiny vacant waiting room to cry.

Like it or not, Meg had grown roots in her mother's crazy venture that strengthened under adversity. For the first time, she felt a sense of purpose. A sense of belonging. And she knew it would hurt to rip her newly grown roots out. Just like it pained to leave Robbie. But this was where she needed to be. She felt certain of that. And whatever the result, she prepared to face it without any personal agenda.

CHAPTER 38

THE DOOR COUNTIAN

Wisconsin's Largest Twice-Weekly Newspaper

Featured Columnist...
Seneca Parks

Wanted: weather-predicting critter

FOR THE FOURTH YEAR IN A ROW, Selwyn Picker's groundhog Fred blew it. His forecast for an early spring was repudiated by an old-fashioned, socko blizzard that struck the peninsula last night, causing the cancellation of all county school houses, stores, and Curly Paul's breakfast social. Selwyn Picker has already offered to demote old Fred to the sausage grinder in favor of a critter with better weather-predicting prowess. And as much as I'm sweet on old Fred, if I thought for one instant that would bring about an early spring, *bon appetite*. Sorry Fred.

In other news, the Coast Guard cutter broke through a record 48 inches of ice to open up the waters of Green Bay to boat traffic.

CHAPTER 39

ST. PADDY'S DAY

Music's in the air, joy is everywhere,
a sea o' green and a rainbow arch,
everyone's Irish on the 17th of March.

—Irish saying

WHEN MEG RETURNED to the post office, Chairman Philpot presented her termination letter from the U.S. Post Office.

"They say you violated some postal regulations," Chairman Philpot apologized. "Something about an unauthorized mail carrier, ay."

The only way the U.S. Post Office would've known is if someone reported her. And Emmie Elefsson's hands were all over this.

"I need this job," Meg knew the shop's survival depended on it.

"And if I was the Post Office, I'd give it to you," Chairman Philpot said. "But I don't get to make the decision. Hey, look on the bright side. This will give you more time to work on that parade of yours, ay."

Meg thoroughly enjoyed upsetting Emmie Elefsson and her Historical Society Nazis, preparing for Door County's inaugural St. Patrick's Day parade. She stuck fliers in everyone's mail (especially the Historical Society ladies). Offered free Irish dance lessons on Wednesday afternoons to help break the winter blahs. Stole a large tractor wagon from Robbie's orchard to use as a parade float. And when Robbie returned the first week of March, she paid a visit to personally hand him a flier.

Anna opened the front door.

A wheelchair sat alongside the living room couch, where someone lay under a blanket.

"Is he sleeping?" Meg asked, a bit startled to find Anna.

"He doesn't want any visitors," Anna said, blocking the doorway. She was being nice. Meg knew the only visitor Robbie didn't want to see was her.

"Alright," Meg smiled, undaunted. "Here then," she handed Anna a green flier, noting dates, times, and places of the St. Patrick's Day parade. "It's Door County's first St. Patrick's parade. Hope you can make it," she said loud enough for Robbie to hear.

Anna read the flier. "Floats…," she noted. "Hey, you didn't borrow a wagon from the barn, did you?"

"No," Meg said with a straight face. Which wasn't exactly a lie, because technically she didn't "borrow," she stole it.

March 17th marked the anniversary of St. Patrick's death, and for centuries, Catholics in Ireland paid homage by attending mass and often wearing a shamrock in his honor.

At the time of Patrick's death in 461 A.D., wearing green was bad luck. Green was believed the favorite color of the fairies. And any superstitious Irishman who dared wear it risked a fairy curse put on them. Patrick wore blue (Ireland's national color at the time). But his proclivity to use shamrocks to explain the Holy Trinity prompted admirers to tuck a sprig of shamrock in their hair or lapel to mark the anniversary of his death, deeming this holy symbol the only safe "wearin' o' the green." Leave it to O'mericans to supersize this homage by pinning shamrocks all over their clothes to loudly proclaim their Irishness, which over the years evolved into wearing green ribbons, green scarves, green clothes, etc. (the fear of Ireland's fairies no match for O'mericans). When the Irish immigrated to America, their annual tribute often continued from the church to the local pub, as an opportunity to drink a few pints with fellow countrymen until the wee hours, spilling back into the streets in a sea of inebriated brotherly love, laughing and slurring songs about their beloved Auld Sod. That was Patrick's enduring legacy.

"The English Protestants bastardized it," Mo spat. Those same oppressors who for centuries seized Irish lands, burned their churches, and hung their necks from the nearest tree, turned their quaint, respectable memorial into today's ridiculous buffoonery. Back in the 18th century, after observing this annual merriment, Mo speculated the city fathers of New York (all WASPs, Mo pointed out bitterly) amused themselves by sanctioning an official St. Patrick's parade as an acceptable excuse to get stinkin' drunk under the guise of acting like Irishmen—which the WASPs further exaggerated by hamming it up in ridiculous green regalia to perpetuate the stereotype.

Mo hated St. Patrick's Day to the core. Patrick himself was a fraud. He was neither Irish, nor named Patrick, nor an officially canonized saint. He was an Englishman named Maewyn Succat. And no true Irishman dared recognize that phony as the country's patron saint.

The only way Mo agreed to take part in Meg's festivities was if it remained true to Irish tradition by starting with a mass and then meandering from the church to a local pub, where they could drink a few scoops and toast to their beloved Ireland. No green beer or Plastic Paddyism. And none of this scheduling the parade the Saturday before (so the local pubs could reap the rewards). It had to be on March 17th. The day the phony died.

"'Tis the only reason the Irish celebrate it," Mo joked. "Because it meant one less Englishman."

Against Mo's wishes, Meg ordered some Plastic Paddy paraphernalia: *Kiss Me I'm Irish* shirts and trinkets, silly green leprechaun hats, shamrock beer huggies, green drinking gloves (with the fingers cut off to allow better grip), glow-in-the-dark shamrock underwear, battery-run plastic earrings in the shape of shamrocks that blinked, shamrock fishnet hose, and big green Mardi Gras-type beads all in the name of fun. When it arrived, you'd swear by Mo's reaction that someone dumped a tipper full of cow manure in the middle of their shop.

"It's just for St. Patrick's Day," Meg tried to talk Mo off the ledge. "This is what customers want. They love this stuff. It makes them happy."

"It makes them look stupid," Mo seethed. She gritted her teeth, and for the first time in memory acquiesced. "Fine!"

Meg was flabbergasted. No battle. No blood bath. For once, Mo put aside her narrow-minded stubbornness without a fight.

"But come March 18th," Mo insisted. "All this is out of me shop."

Meg agreed.

In addition to promoting the parade around town, Meg contacted several area TV stations to tout the monumental event.

A week before the parade, the same Green Bay news crew who shot a piece on Meg's lutefisk entry, telephoned to tape a small interest story on Mo.

"I will in me hat," Mo refused to participate in such shameless self-promotion.

"It's the first St. Patrick's parade in Door County history," Meg insisted. "It's not self-promotion, it's news."

"St. Patrick was a phony!" Mo spat, muffling her temper before it blew.

When the news van arrived, Meg held her breath, fearing what her insubordinate mother might say. But the moment the cameraman and reporter stepped into the shop, Mo charmed their blood green (or blue, as she preferred).

"You know, we have a sayin': 'There are no strangers in Ireland.' Anytime someone shows up on our doorstep, we find somethin' special to offer them to eat with a cup o' tea," she handed out fresh-baked soda bread much to their delighted palates.

Mo entertained them with charming quips, funny anecdotes, superstitions, Irish magic, and when she finished an hour later, they didn't want to leave. Before they departed, the reporter bought a lovely pair of Claddagh earrings for his mother-in-law, a *Kiss Me I'm Irish* button, and a warm Aran sweater for himself. The cameraman bought two pairs of Irish drinking gloves and a pair of glow-in-the-dark shamrock boxers for their boss.

"Glad that's over with," Mo bristled after they left.

Meg smiled at her mother's bogus exasperation, knowing anytime Mo spewed Irishness like that, she enjoyed herself immensely.

The news piece aired the following evening and the shop's phone started ringing with viewers asking for directions.

The Irish shop enjoyed the best week of sales in its short history. New customers visited all the way from Green Bay, Manitowoc, and Oshkosh. Locals stopped in to rub elbows with their newest celebrity. And several guests found the "perfect dress" in Meg's own design collection, which gave Meg the most pleasure of all.

Mo's fifteen minutes of fame escalated her to a whole new level of Irishness amongst the new influx of customers, dishing out blarney like raw fish to clapping seals. By week's end, she partook in all the Plastic Paddyism, hamming it up in a pair of shamrock fishnet hose (which she sold the lot of). And for once in her life, she left her Irish snobbery on the shelf and enjoyed the ridiculous pageantry of St. Paddy's Day.

At mid-week, Booker Wade paraded up to the counter

with a *Kiss Me I'm Irish* T-shirt and a gloating grin.

"Not a word!" Mo warned.

Booker cackled. "Saw you on TV"

"I niver watch TV" Mo placed Booker's purchases in a bag as she turned to the calculator to add his total.

"You looked good," Booker stared with a wolfy grin. "Real good. How 'bout after this parade, you and I go out for some corned beef. Maybe see if there was one snake St. Patrick didn't drive out of Ireland."

"I have a weddin' ring on me finger," Mo flashed her gold band. "'Tis disrespectful!" she thrust the bag at him. "Besides, corned beef is about as Irish as that ridiculous shirt you just bought."

Booker cackled. "Nice hose by the way," he motioned at her fishnet shamrock hose, waving as he walked out the door with a *ring-a-ling-ling*.

Meg stepped over to an agitated Mo. "He didn't pay again, did he?"

Mo looked down at her calculator. She forgot. "Shite!"

"I'm thinking all your flirting with him is distracting you," Meg teased.

"The man's a gobshite!" Mo tossed out the Irish slang for "utterly obnoxious fool."

"You like him," Meg grinned.

"I do in me hat!"

"You DO like him!" Meg lit up. "He's Pierce Brosnan…"

" — Shut your gob!" Mo snapped and walked away.

"He IS Pierce Brosnan," Meg laughed.

Mo used to make such a big show about how much she

hated the Irish actor Pierce Brosnan, vociferously refusing to watch any of his movies, until Mary Lou discovered a hidden cache of the Irish actor's DVDs in Mo's closet, including all five seasons of *Remington Steele*.

"Pierce Brosnan!" Meg gloated.

Meg called Caitlyn that night to chinwag about Mo's secret crush, and the bouncy news fell on flat ears. Caitlyn sounded depressed. "I'm fine," she insisted, "Just tired," then shifted the conversation to questions about Meg and Robbie.

"Come to Door County," Meg urged. "Come for the parade. Bring the girls. It'll be fun!"

"I can't. They have school. I have to work…"

"Come anyway. You know you want to see Mo in fishnet shamrock hose."

Meg sensed a smile over the phone. "Mary Lou's coming," she waved another carrot. "Me and my Irish dance troupe are even going to dance." Another carrot.

"Your Irish dance troupe?" Caitlyn was shocked.

"I've been giving lessons. I have three students."

"You've been giving lessons?" Caitlyn couldn't believe it.

"Come on. We're all going to dance in the parade. Me, Mo, Mary Lou…"

"Mo and Mary Lou!" Caitlyn chuckled.

"It'll be a riot. Come on. Do it with us. You and the girls. We can use all the Irish people we can get. We even made a float."

"You made a float!" Caitlyn perked up. "What is it?"

"You'll have to come to find out."

They chinwagged a bit longer, Meg even elicited a few

laughs, and before they hung up, Caitlyn left the visit at a "We'll see."

Meg knew she wouldn't come.

"Love you," Meg said.

"Love you," Caitlyn said appreciatively. "Thanks. I needed to laugh."

Mo prepared the traditional St. Patrick's Day meal—boiled bacon (or "rashers" as she called them) and cabbage. No corned beef. Back in Ireland, no commoner could afford beef. Not until they immigrated to America where beef preserved in salt corns (corned beef) was cheaper than pork did they switch diets.

Mary Lou drove up with George and her 17-year-old adopted daughter Grace, who pushed Mary Lou to wits end. Over wine, the New England matron commiserated with Mo and Meg about Grace's new boyfriend.

"He's going to get her pregnant!" she worried. "She is so stupid. She's worse than you ever were," she said to Meg.

"Thank you," Meg laughed.

"This guy's a total loser. First off, he's three years older than her. Dropped out of high school. No job. And wears these stupid black outfits with this ridiculous cowboy hat, like he thinks he's Jesse James or something. Teddy's his name. And then she tells me the other day he got his last girlfriend pregnant. Use your goddamn brain! She is so stupid. She is SO stupid!"

St. Patrick's Day fell on a Thursday, and the weather proved so bitterly cold, you could watch your breath crystallize and fall to the ground. The chill froze flesh instantly, forcing them to hide their St. Patrick's garb under thick Eskimo-like layers.

Mo, Meg, Mary Lou, George, Grace, and Meg's three students—a mom and 10-year-old twin girls—comprised the entire parade.

They attended morning mass at Whitefish Creek's Catholic church, then stepped into the biting cold, where the float awaited.

They built a small, 4-foot-high thatched-roof cottage mockup on one side and a Blarney Castle mockup on the other. Speakers blasted Irish jigs. A humungous Irish flag flew off the back. And the trailer provided enough room in the middle for Mo, Meg, Mary Lou, Hat Guy and Meg's students to dance some jigs, while George and a frumpy Grace towed the trailer in the Yukon.

When they pulled onto the parade route, it looked like a ghost town.

Waiting at the start, Sheriff Baldy Bridenhagen and Chairman Philpot sat in Baldy's heated patrol car, wished them well, and following regulations, trailed the float about 30 yards back to prevent "traffic" from passing.

A single spectator stood on the route. Booker Wade wore his *Kiss Me I'm Irish* shirt, drank from a flask, and whistled and cheered them on as they passed, "Hey, how 'bout some beads!" He grinned and ogled Mo the whole way, making a jealous Hat Guy uncomfortable.

"Gobshite," Mo muttered at Booker.

"Pierce Brosnan," Meg smiled.

"Shut your gob!"

A few shopkeepers poked their heads into the bone-chilling air as the parade route moved down Main Street.

Emmie Elefsson peeked out of her Whitefish Creek Mercantile, shaking her head in disapproval, with her black Labrador Flowers at her side.

As they turned the last corner of the route, they viewed the final few empty blocks to the Whitefish Creek Grill and Meg's heart sank at not seeing Robbie.

He never came.

The last week, she entertained grand scenarios of Robbie showing up and proclaiming how foolish he was. Then they'd kiss, and he'd give her trouble about stealing his trailer. Now she felt foolish, left to doubt whether his old self would ever show again. And that cold reality lodged in her stomach like a sharp, depressing pit.

As they approached the parade route's end, an unmistakable figure in a huge beaver coat stood in the shadows of the Whitefish Creek Grill.

Alewife Alma. Meg recognized her instantly.

Meg's insides flooded with warmth, overwhelmed by the gesture of this odd hermit who walked miles in the freezing cold to offer support and snag a pair of cheap green beads.

Despite the absence of paradegoers, they all enjoyed themselves tremendously, acting the fool, hamming it up, and as they pulled in front of the Whitefish Creek Grill for beers, Mo and Mary Lou toasted Meg's inaugural efforts, vowing an even grander parade next year.

Meg only wished her sister was with them.

CHAPTER 40

GOBSMACKED

Each day has enough trouble of its own to worry about tomorrow.

—Irish saying

CAITLYN CALLED FOR A FULL REPORT of the parade later that afternoon, and announced her plans to visit the second week of April. In another string of good news, the shop made enough money to pay that month's mortgage—thanks to that glorious Irish fraud St. Patrick. Unfortunately for the shop, St. Patrick's only came once a year.

The next day, Meg drove to Robbie's. When no one answered, she left gifts inside the screen door—a green leprechaun hat and drinking gloves—and a note:

Missed your jig at the parade.

A week later, she returned to find the house empty again. She wrote another note, and left fresh-baked raisin bread with *Jesus* strips hidden inside.

Enjoy! ☺

At the end of the week, she returned again and saw Robbie using a walker. He stepped gingerly with his new prosthetics, his leg movements stiff and unbalanced, like walking on short stilts for the first time. Then he abandoned the walker to take a few independent steps, lost balance, and fell to the dirt.

"Damn it!" he cursed, struggling to get up.

"You okay?" Meg approached with a big blue *All Things Irish* shopping bag.

Robbie struggled to stand on his prosthetic feet and escape her approach. "I told you I don't want you here."

"I just stopped by. Let me help you."

"No. I don't need help. I need to learn this myself."

"Where's Anna?"

Robbie propped himself up on his knees, then stuck out his right prosthetic-filled tennis shoe to find solid footing. Meg secretly rooted for him as he slowly lifted his body onto his new prosthetic feet. She wanted to applaud and embrace him, but restrained.

"California," Robbie finally answered with a grunt.

"She left?"

"I sent her home."

Meg was pleasantly taken aback. "Why?"

"What do you want?"

"Nothing. Just stopped by to see you."

"Well you've seen me."

"Your nose is an improvement from the old one," Meg

teased, observing the reconstructed feature.

Robbie's prosthetics made him taller.

"Those new feet add a good three inches," Meg noted. "A lot of people would kill for that."

Robbie said nothing.

"I was at Lighthouse Island last week," Meg smiled. "Ice is getting thinner."

"Were you looking for something specific?" Robbie demanded.

"My sister's coming next week. So I won't be able to bother you or drop off notes. So don't miss me. Oh. And I brought you this." It was a blanket. "I knitted it myself. And some raisin bread."

The two stood there in each other's presence, both wanting to say something, but neither able.

"Alright," Meg smiled. "I'll be back to bother you in a week."

Meg walked back to her car. As she popped the door, Robbie shouted. "How's your sister doing?"

"Her last scan was clear."

"Good."

Meg smiled. "It is good."

Their gaze lingered. Then Robbie motioned towards the raisin bread in the bag. "You know, the last one you baked me had paper in it."

Meg grinned with her whole face. This one did too.

Caitlyn arrived at the Door the next day without the girls. She looked tired, wore a Notre Dame ball cap, her hair started to grow back, and she actually gained a few pounds.

Not much, but a few.

They played cards at night over beers and crisps. Laughed a lot. Walked on the beach. Reminisced about old times. Watched all the classic Irish movies: *It's a Wonderful Life* (about an upright Irish family); *Gone With The Wind* (featuring the greatest Irish heroine in cinematic history); and *Darby O'Gill and the Little People* (a Disneyized version of leprechauns that Mo abhorred—so naturally Meg relished).

Caitlyn loved any movie that served up a grand happy ending. Especially love stories that closed with the couple marrying, having babies, and living happily ever after. Meg called those "Caitlyn Endings." Anything short was like ordering a sundae and receiving a bowl of ordinary vanilla ice cream. Even if it ended with the couple's wedding, if it didn't show them with children and all their loose ends tied up in a bow of happiness, it wasn't a Caitlyn Ending. Plain and simple. Marriage, kids, bow of happiness. Caitlyn Ending.

During her visit, some of their siblings drove up, and of course Mary Lou wasn't about to miss the fun.

"I'll bet it was hard leaving the girls," their brother Danny said over a card game of Sheep's Head.

"They don't miss me," Caitlyn said. "It doesn't make any difference."

It broke everyone's heart to hear her speak like that.

The entire week Nick never called, never wrote, never had the girls send drawings or cards, nothing. It was so sad. The reality of the situation was devastating.

On the warmest evening of her stay, the sisters wrapped themselves under their great-grandmother's blanket, sat outside the Irish shop, and gazed at the heavens as they did in their childhood. They wove their arms and legs around each other like the cable knit of an Aran sweater, searching for satellites and shooting stars.

"The girls have a *feis* in August," Caitlyn said. "It's Mary's first one. Can you come up? It would mean so much to her."

"Sure."

"Will you make sure you do?" Caitlyn squeezed Meg's hand. "It'd be nice having you. For me, too," she smiled sincerely.

Meg embraced her with a smile of her own. "I will. I promise."

The two sisters relished their renewed bond, squeezing each other tight, as they spent the night counting shooting stars until they fell asleep in each other's company, just like they did as kids.

"Meg," Caitlyn shook her awake amidst the early morning dew and breaking dawn.

"What," Meg sprung up, thinking the worst.

"I caught him," Caitlyn grinned.

"What?" Meg rubbed her heavy eyelids, pulling the blanket tighter in the chill of the morning.

"Your poop bandit."

"What?" Meg needed coffee.

"The one you were telling me about over the summer. The thing that left all those poops behind the shop."

"You caught it?" Meg snapped to full alert. "What was it? What is it?"

Caitlyn pointed down Main Street. "I saw it over there. Around 4:30 or so. It walked right up and went behind the shop. Sure enough, when I went back there, it was in the bushes pooping. It looked right at me too. Didn't even spook. Then it pranced right back down Main Street — "

" — What was it?"

"A black Lab," Caitlyn grinned. "I followed it all the way down Main Street and watched it go to the front door of the Whitefish Creek Mercantile — "

" — Emmie Elefsson," Meg stewed. "Her dog Flowers."

"Yep," Caitlyn beamed. "I saw her in her robe giving it a treat. She saw me too. Looked nervous."

"I'll bet she trained that damn dog to do that. She's been sabotaging us the whole time. You wouldn't believe how bad it smelled this summer — "

" — I'm sure."

"Do you know how many customers that kept away?" Meg seethed.

"I know. Here," Caitlyn handed Meg a shovel. "I got an idea."

Later that morning, as Emmie Elefsson readied the Mercantile for her customers, a clunk echoed on her roof. She stopped. Another clunk above. Then another, and another, and what sounded like a riddle of bullets falling from the sky. She glanced out the window and saw Meg and Caitlyn with a wheelbarrow filled with manure, catapulting the frozen dookie onto her roof with shovels.

"What are you doing! Have you lost your mind? Stop! Stop!" she rushed outside, waving furiously.

"Just returning what's yours," Meg shouted, as they both catapulted shovelfuls.

The two sisters laughed.

Emmie screamed at them. "Stop! I won't be able to get that down!"

"Here, catch!" Meg slung one at her.

Emmie screamed as it hit her porch. "I'm calling the sheriff!"

Meg flicked another as Emmie fled inside, and laughing, turned to find Caitlyn doubled over.

"Cait," Meg rushed to her.

Caitlyn smiled faintly. "All the chemo. Still don't have my old energy. Take me back inside," Caitlyn's voice strained.

They never returned to their wheelbarrow.

Caitlyn spent the last few days on the couch with her nose in a book.

"I love you," the sisters parted, this time not letting go of one another at the airport until the last call for boarding.

"Love you."

And Mo embraced Caitlyn as she did Meg's departure for Ireland, handing Caitlyn a rosary of St. Brigid to pray on the flight back to Boston.

CHAPTER 41

MURPHY'S LAW

Whatever can go wrong will, and at the worst possible time.

—Irish saying

THE BANK AUDITED THE SHOP after Emmie Elefsson informed them about the change in Meg's employment status with the U.S. Post Office. When Meg became delinquent on the May mortgage, the bank called their note, with 30 days to pay before they sold the property to "another interested party," which meant Emmie Elefsson and her Door County Historical Society cronies somehow raised enough money to cut a deal with the bank.

"You can't fight God's will," Mo said. "I guess we'll see about the bank's."

In the ensuing days and weeks, Robbie all but disappeared. His boat *The Osprey* lay anchored at Sister Bay's fishing dock. He kept away from the winery. He spent most of his days in physical therapy down in Sturgeon Bay, returning to Milwaukee several times for fittings of his customized prosthetics. And for the first time in over sixteen years he declined to play master fish boiler at the upcoming Fyr Bal Festival, much to everyone's sadness.

Rumors abounded about Robbie holing up on Lighthouse Island or Alewife Alma's hermitage. And after numerous home visits with no luck, Meg took the Fitzgibbons's 20-foot Sea Ray out of winter storage and docked at Lighthouse Island. Still no Robbie. She climbed the tower and gazed over the vast sparkling lake. A large freighter moved along the horizon on this picture-perfect, blue sky day. She wished a few clouds appeared as the sun descended, knowing the sunset would not reach its full potential without the imperfect billows to compliment its spectrum of light.

An ache tightened her stomach. She worried about Robbie. The hole his absence left whistled like a hollow log in the wind.

The one time they saw each other since Caitlyn's visit, Meg was returning from yet another bank who declined to purchase their note (this one in Green Bay), and they passed on the road. Meg honked and stopped. And in her rearview mirror, she watched Robbie slow, hoping he'd make a U-turn, but he just offered a faint wave and drove on.

When her thoughts weren't filled with Caitlyn or Robbie, Meg schemed to keep the shop alive. She pleaded with the bank to extend their grace period through the lucrative summer season.

Ring-a-ling-ling.

The jingle of the entry bell fell on deaf ears as Meg stood behind the shop's counter absorbing the bank's grim answer—a Notice of Foreclosure.

"Hello?" a man said.

Meg remained buried in the notice's "vacating the premises" language by "August 1." A month away.

"Hello?" the man repeated an octave higher, leaning into Meg's peripheral view.

Meg glanced up preoccupied, and startled at the sight of a handsome, thirtyish man smiling at her. Meg's morose gaze softened. "Hi."

"Hi," he smiled bigger, a bit nervous. It was sweet. He looked about mid-thirties, tall, fit, and sharp in his navy polo and khaki pants.

"Can I help you look for something?" Meg perked up.

"Is this your shop?"

"It's my mother's."

"Is she around?"

"No."

"I guess I should give this to you then," the man held out an envelope.

"What is it?" Meg asked skeptically before touching it, not wanting to be served another creditor's notice.

"My mother was here a while back," he said. "She bought a bunch of stuff, and I guess forgot her purse. This is what she owed."

"That was last summer," Meg accepted the envelope and opened it.

"She passed away."

"I'm sorry."

"She had leukemia. She'd been fighting it for years. She always loved Door County. She spent her summers here as a child. She said those were some of her happiest years."

Meg opened the envelope and her eyes popped from her head when she saw the check.

"It's for three thousand dollars," Meg exclaimed. "This isn't right. It's way too much."

"She wanted you to have that."

"I can't," Meg held it out. "Here, let me grab the books. I'll find out exactly how much."

"It's not like she can write you another check," he chuckled.

The silly notion gave her pause.

The man smiled. "When mom came home that evening, she was a new person. She invited everyone over for dinner: kids, spouses, grandkids. Cooked. Joked. Gave out presents. She was so happy. I hadn't seen her like that in years. None of us had. Some of the grandkids only knew her as a sick, tired old woman until that night. And every time we asked what got into her, she went on about your shop and how wonderful you were to trust her like that. She said it restored her faith in people. I can't thank you enough for that. It gave us back our mom, even if just for a night. Whatever she wrote that check for, no amount of money could match what you gave us."

Meg was speechless.

"I'm sorry it took so long to pay you back. She slipped into a coma a few days after that night and died in August."

"I'm sorry," Meg said.

"She died at peace. We didn't realize you were never paid until we found this check tucked in one of her books."

Meg was still speechless. "Let me cash it and give you the rest back."

"No. She wanted you to have it. Consider it interest."

Meg attempted to give it back, but he refused.

"Thank you," Meg smiled. "This couldn't have come at a better time."

"Then she'd be glad," he smiled into her eyes. "I'm Kevin by the way. Kevin Reed."

They shook hands.

"Meg McKenna."

"Nice to meet you Meg McKenna."

"You too, Kevin Reed."

"You know, I'm up here for the weekend. I just drove up from Chicago. I don't know anyone. Would you care to have dinner with me?"

Meg startled. "Tonight? You know it's the big Fyr Bal Festival. Everyone's at the fish boil."

"I'm not a fish guy. I had my fill of Catholic fish fries growing up. What time do you close your shop?"

"Around nine."

"Can I pick you up then?"

Meg hesitated.

"I'm sorry," Kevin said. "I should probably be smoother. I've never been very good at this. I usually stumble over my own tongue."

"You're fine, it's just...I can't. I'm sort of with someone."

"Ah," Kevin apologized. "I didn't see any Claddagh or anything..."

"You know that?" Meg was impressed.

"Big Irish Catholic family," he smiled. "Youngest of six. Only one still single. And don't think I don't hear it."

"Me too," Meg felt a bond. "Are you guys Domers?"

"Everyone but me. My mother never forgave me for picking UMKC over Notre Dame. But they had a 6-year med program."

"You're a doctor?"

"Cardio-surgeon at University of Chicago," he smiled. "I barely see my own apartment, let alone social settings. Please forgive me. Well, whoever he is, he's a very lucky man."

"Thanks," Meg smiled.

"Here's my card if you ever need any cardio work, heart checked, anything like that," he handed her his card. "I make house calls. I guess that's my not-too-subtle attempt at a Hail Mary pass in case things don't work out between the two of you."

"Yeah, I saw that," Meg smiled.

"Thought you did," he conceded. "It was nice to meet you, Meg McKenna."

"You too, Kevin Reed. I'm sorry, *Doctor* Reed."

"You saw how I slipped that in there too," he conceded sheepishly.

"Good try, though. Almost subtle enough."

"I need to get out more," he smiled, then took his leave.

He left Meg with a big grin on her face and a light air that briefly lifted the dark cloud of foreclosure notices. A grin she wore right into the bank that afternoon to pay off a part of their delinquent June mortgage.

"Give us until the end of summer," she pleaded. "It's barely June. You know how big July and August are. We'll be able to get current on everything."

"And then we're back in the same situation this winter,"

the bank director, Fordel Hogenson, apologized. "You're still behind four months of payments. I'm sorry. There's nothing more I can do. Emmie Elefsson is ready to buy the note. You can always try to work out some rental agreement with them."

"They've wanted us out of here from day one and you know it, Ford. Come on. Please."

"I'm sorry. The directors have already decided. They're selling all our bad notes. The bank needs cash. The only reason we've strung it out this long is because the Historical Society didn't lock down all their funding until now, and it took a little bit to process all the paperwork. I'm sorry. Unless you can come up with the outstanding balance on the note…"

" — Three hundred thousand dollars!"

"I'm sorry, there's nothing more I can do."

"This isn't right, Ford."

Ford's sincere eyes echoed his apology. "I never said it was right. I just said it was business."

Two weeks later, the bank auctioned off the little Irish shop at the top of Main Street. It sold for a loss to Emmie Elefsson and her Door County Historical Society.

The loss from the sale eliminated Mo's equity. A hundred thousand dollars worth. Not to mention the tens of thousands of dollars she spent renovating it.

Mo and her late husband Jimmy had taken out so many loans and second and third mortgages to pay for all their children's Catholic high school and college from what Meg ascertained, they saved little for themselves. When Mo sold their St. Louis home, all the money went to pay off loans.

And even then, she dipped into her savings to become solvent. Whatever remained, Mo used to purchase the shop, renovate it, and stock with over $50,000 worth of inventory.

Meg failed to grasp the extent of Mo's dire financial situation until the foreclosure. Her parents gave everything to the kids' education. Over a million dollars. And never once thought about their own wellbeing or financial future. Education was the priority. Along with instilling Mo's cherished Irish culture. It's how they said "I love you."

And Meg · ignorantly shunned it all—just to be belligerent.

Meg and Mo ran a going-out-of-business sale.

On August 1, they sadly boxed the last of Mo's talismans and charms, all her Irish frames, and whatever didn't sell. They removed the Irish flag from the front entrance, took down her lucky horseshoe and thrush cross of St. Brigid, picked up her *Cead Mile Failte* welcome mat, unhooked the wooden front sign that said *All Things Irish*, and sadly abandoned the dream. Mo filled two bedrooms at Mary Lou's summer home with the boxes, and then met this hardship with resolute faith.

"'Tis all part of our journey," she reassured Meg.

Meg took the foreclosure much harder, watching the final nail in their coffin when the Historical Society painted over its crazy orange-white-and-green tri-stripes in red.

CHAPTER 42

FEIS

May God grant you many years to live,
for sure He must be knowing,
the earth has angels all too few,
and heaven is overflowing.

—Irish blessing

CAITLYN APPEARED GAUNT and tired, her eyes more sallow, when Meg, Mo, and Mary Lou arrived in Boston for the girls' August *feis*.

The morning of the event, Mo readied the outfits and big, curly wigs, just as she prepared Meg and Caitlyn years ago. Mary Lou helped cook the food for the deluge of post-feis guests. And Meg asked Nick to drive her to a florist to purchase some shamrocks and flowers for the girls.

As Meg stood at the cashier's with two bouquets, she observed Nick slip out the store carrying two beautiful potted flowers without paying. It caught Meg off guard. Was he so distraught it slipped his mind? But when she returned to the car, Nick laughed about shoplifting the plants. It was truly bizarre, making Meg wonder what her sister endured all these years. Sadly, Nick was no longer the kindly person she remembered from their old apartment days in St. Louis.

The girls looked beautiful in their curly wigs, white blouses, and purple skirts, with embroidery stitched by Caitlyn. Little Mary simply bubbled at the prospect of attending her first feis, while Megan seemed snippy, especially at Caitlyn.

Meg, Mo, and Mary Lou joined Nick's family, who seemed less than enthused about this silly Irish dancing cult.

"Why don't they take ballet?" Nick's mother voiced. "It's so much more beautiful."

A large hotel in downtown Boston hosted the feis, with all ten of its conference rooms accommodating the thousands of people who crammed in, vying for limited seating. Nick's family never witnessed anything like it as they maneuvered their way through the packed halls.

"These people can't all be here for this silly Irish dancing?" Nick's mother couldn't believe it.

Irish dancing was an entire subculture, part beauty pageant, part dancing, part Irish pedigree. The girls wore thousand dollar dresses that bore the colors and symbols of their dance school. The more advanced wore unique dresses, embroidered with all kinds of beautiful Celtic weaves and designs, usually imported from Ireland at costs in upwards of $5,000. Their giant, curly wigs cost hundreds of dollars. And Irish vendors lined the hotel corridors catering to all the O'mericans' voracious Irish appetites.

Meg found herself critiquing their wares alongside Mo: "I like that," "Don't like that," "That's lovely," or "No self-respecting Irishmen would sell such gaudy trinkets."

She had become her mother.

Meg overheard conversations amongst the parents jockeying over who notched more visits to Ireland, who boasted greater Irish ancestry, whose children attended Notre Dame; they compared dance schools and dresses, rankings and trophies; critiqued judges and competitors; and some parents shouted pep talks at their children, rivaling the pre-battle cries at D-Day. Competitive soccer moms were kittens compared to Irish dance moms.

Meg relished the chance of watching her nieces dance. Mary was a natural just like her. She took first place in the hornpipe and beamed with happiness at her first-ever trophy. When everyone lauded the little protégée's accomplishment, Meg glimpsed her sister secreting herself in a corner to discreetly wipe tears from her eyes.

"You okay?" Meg approached in private.

Caitlyn startled, thinking no one was watching. She pushed a smile, wiping the last tears from her red eyes. "It's back," she confided sadly.

Meg's heart sank, knowing she meant the cancer.

"How can you say that?"

"I feel it. I just wanted to be here for the girls, not in some hospital."

Meg was speechless. "When is your next scan?"

"It doesn't matter," Caitlyn smiled bravely. "Don't say anything," she asked. "Just let me enjoy today."

They waited another hour for Megan's first dance. Meg said nothing about her sister's condition, although inside, her heart broke.

"They moved it to Suite B," Mo announced the change to Megan's schedule. "It's all the way at the other end of the hotel, the next floor."

"Let me sit down for a minute," Caitlyn sounded exhausted.

"Are you sick again!" Megan accused her mother.

"Mommy just needs to rest her feet. I'll be fine."

Caitlyn later watched Megan take fourth place in the hornpipe. When she went to embrace her oldest daughter, Megan broke away, upset with the outcome.

"I did horrible," Megan cursed herself. "I didn't win a trophy."

"You can have mine," Mary offered sweetly.

"Keep it," Megan snapped at her younger sister. "It's just a stupid trophy."

Her callous words crushed her little sister's accomplishment.

"Come on," Megan tugged her mother's hand. "I need to hurry. The slip jig is in Suite D. My teacher says we need to run down there. Come on!"

"Megan," Meg motioned, concerned for Caitlyn's health. "Come on, we'll run ahead. They can catch up."

Megan stared loathingly at her mother, as if she were just being lazy.

"I'm coming," Caitlyn stood on weak legs.

"Come on!" Megan urged. "You're gonna make me late."

Caitlyn smiled sweetly at her daughter, and they walked down the long winding corridor to Suite D.

Megan's final dance earned a first-place trophy and Caitlyn gave her an enormous hug, though Megan acted nonchalant.

When Meg, Caitlyn, Mo, Mary Lou and the girls reached the parking lot, they discovered their minivan boxed in by a double-parked SUV.

"Get in the car," Meg commanded, taking the driver's seat for an off-road adventure.

The girls laughed when their "wild" aunt Meg drove onto the sidewalk, honked off a few startled walkers, and finally bumped over a curb back to the street. It was the biggest laugh Caitlyn shared with her girls since her diagnosis. And Meg knew the delight in the girls' eyes meant the world to Caitlyn.

That evening, Caitlyn played hostess extraordinaire, talking and joking and making sure Nick's enormous family received enough food and drinks. She even started washing dishes until Meg and Mary Lou shooed her away, admonishing her to enjoy her daughters.

Caitlyn and her girls continued to laugh all night, feeding off each other, dancing jigs to the delight of all, and in those precious hours, Megan and Mary enjoyed a glimpse of their old mom.

Meg failed to recall a time she admired her sister more.

The next morning, the girls rushed into Caitlyn's room hoping to laugh and play with their mom, only to discover Caitlyn too weak and sick to get out of bed, despite her heart's desire.

The following day, Caitlyn admitted herself into the hospital after an excruciating night of pain and vomiting blood. They discovered tumors throughout her body, with no hope of operation.

"I want you to promise something," she told Meg, Mo,

and Mary Lou in the privacy of her hospital room. "Don't say anything bad about Nick. He'll be the gatekeeper between you and the girls. If you alienate him, he could make it very difficult for you to see them. So promise me. No matter what happens. You need to do whatever it takes to stay in their lives. Even if it's to my detriment. I don't care. Kiss his ass..."

"What did he do to you?" Meg asked sadly.

"Just promise you'll do whatever it takes to stay in their lives. I need to know that," Caitlyn urged.

Mo and Mary Lou conceded.

"Fine," Meg reluctantly agreed, even though it burned her to think Nick was getting away with all this. "Nick should have cancer, not you," Meg boiled. "Why you? Why you, Cait?"

"Why not me," Caitlyn said.

The startling answer stopped Meg cold.

"Are any of us so special?" Caitlyn said. "Just keep praying. Pray whatever God wants us to learn from this, we can learn without me having to die. I'm not ready to leave my girls," she choked.

"How could any God let this happen?" Meg angered.

"Because people are stupid," Mo interrupted. "'Tis the same reason there's poverty, wars, and disease. Sufferin' cleanses us from all the shite in this world. It makes us realize what's really important—helping each other. But of course we're too stupid and wrapped up in the wrong things to take heed very long, and we get caught right back up in all the nonsense until some other tragedy hits. God might as well be whistlin' jigs to a millstone."

"But why Cait? Why do these things happen to the best people?"

"Because no one gives a shite about arseholes," Mo said. "Some right bollix dies, we say 'good riddance.' A good person suffers, we reflect. Maybe people who know Caitlyn take stock in what's really important. Maybe they'll hug their kids more. Maybe they'll help someone they normally wouldn't. Maybe, if just fer a little while, they'll stop bein' in such a hurry for all the wrong things."

Silence settled amongst them.

Meg wanted to say more to her sister. She wanted to thank Caitlyn for all her letters and phone calls when she was at St. Brigid's all those years ago. She wanted to thank her for driving back from Notre Dame to stand at her side when she confronted Mo about her pregnancy. She wanted to thank her for that wonderful year in her apartment when Meg needed independence. She wanted to apologize for ever allowing their relationship to drift apart. For all the years they lost being together. And for what? The reasons seemed meaningless now. She wanted to tell her so many different things, and started to, until Caitlyn cut her off.

"Think it's time we arm wrestle for the Claddagh?" Caitlyn smiled to Meg the first time they found a moment alone.

"No," Meg refused to think about it.

"I need to give it away while I'm still alive. That's tradition." Caitlyn started to slip the beautiful gold ring off her finger.

Meg stopped her. "You still can beat this. You have to. What will I do without a big sister? You keep that ring. I don't want it."

Caitlyn felt too weak to fight. "Then I need to ask a favor."

"Anything."

"The roll-top desk in our living room. In the bottom drawer. There's a shoebox. Inside are birthday cards. For the girls. I wrote them up to their twenty-first birthday. There's also ones for First Communion, graduation, their weddings…" Caitlyn's voice choked at the thought of missing their weddings.

"Could you mail one each year?" Caitlyn smiled. "I put little stickies, so you'll know which birthday."

Meg's throat tightened, making it impossible to squeeze out a word. All she could do was nod and hope Caitlyn couldn't see her heart breaking.

"Thank you," Caitlyn smiled faintly. "I just want them to know I never forgot them."

Their eyes glistened with tears.

Mo and Mary Lou entered the room.

"Okay, too much seriousness," Caitlyn smiled softly. "So this Irish man shows up in a pub one day and orders three pints of Guinness…

"Come on, you know you're going to miss these when I'm gone," Caitlyn grinned infectiously.

They couldn't help but smile, even under this sad reality, because yes, they would miss hearing Caitlyn's Irish jokes. And they settled in, savoring this farewell performance.

"Okay, so this Irishman orders three pints and takes sips from each glass until they're empty, then calls the bartender for three more. The bartender says, 'Sure it's up to yerself, but wouldn't you rather I bring them one at a time? Then they'll be fresh and cold.' 'Nah...' says the man, 'I'm preferrin' ye bring 'em tree at a time. You see, me and me two brothers used to meet at a pub and have good times. Now one is in Australia, the other's in the States, and I'm here. We agreed before we split up that we'd drink to each other's honor this way.' 'Well,' says the bartender, 'that's a grand thing to do. Let me bring yer three pints then.' So this goes on for months. And all the regulars come to know the man's ritual of ordering three pints at a time. Then one day, he comes in and orders only two pints. Everyone goes quiet, figuring something happened to one of his brothers. Then a group of regulars corner the bartender and finally persuade him to find out what happened. So with a heavy heart, the bartender brings the two pints and says, 'Here's your pints...and let me offer my sincerest condolences. What happened?' The Irishman looks extremely puzzled for a moment, then starts laughing. 'Oh, no, no, no! 'Tis nothin' like that. You see, I've given up drinkin' for Lent..."

Everyone laughed through tears. It was just the right levity to break the heavy air. They would miss her jokes dearly.

The last conversation Meg had with her sister was about making Chocolate Oirish Taters. They laughed about their crazy concoction as kids, using the potato pancake mix as an excuse to eat chocolate syrup. And Caitlyn lamented never making the fun concoction with her girls.

"I don't want to be scared of death," Caitlyn divulged. "When my time comes, I want to die at peace. I want to be able to let go. I have to believe that's right. That my girls will be okay. That this will prepare them for something in their future—maybe help them help someone else. I have to believe that. It's just so hard letting go. It's so hard," she broke down. "I don't know if I can do it. I love my girls so much…" she trailed off in tears.

Meg held her sister tight, reassuring her they'd be here, not ever wanting to let go, and they wept together, not saying a word. Caitlyn slipped into a coma that night.

One of her last acts was succumbing to Nick's badgering about giving a taped testimony to lawyers. Nick convinced her the money from a malpractice suit would help pay for medical bills and the girls' education. So for her daughters' future, she acquiesced.

Mo and Meg remained at Caitlyn's side, sleeping in a cot alongside her hospital bed, praying the rosary, and hoping Caitlyn would regain consciousness to talk about her wishes for the girls.

Two weeks later, hooked to all kinds of tubes and monitors, surrounded by Meg and Mo, and a sleeping Nick, mother and daughter watched Caitlyn's heart rate beat to a stop.

As nurses and hospital staff attempted to revive her, they knew she was gone.

For the first time, Caitlyn departed without a final "I love you."

And both Mo and Meg buried themselves in each other's trembling arms and began to cry and cry and cry, not knowing if they'd ever stop crying.

CHAPTER 43

AN IRISH FAREWELL

God's help is nearer than the door.

—Irish saying

THE UNOFFICIAL REPORT WAS over 1,000 people. At one point, parked cars lined five-square blocks around the funeral home in their old St. Louis suburb of Kirkwood. People came from all over the United States and other parts of the world (Germany, Canada, Iceland, France and China). People who wanted to pay their respects and convey their stories about how Caitlyn touched them in some way. Some funny, some sweet, others profoundly moving, but everyone had a story.

A barrage of old high school and grade school friends appeared. A sea of Domers rolled in from across the country to pay their respects for their fallen friend. Colleagues and classmates from Washington University and Harvard paid tribute. A Noble laureate flew in from Germany. One old high school friend drove 26 hours from her teaching post on an Indian reservation in Montana. Word of Caitlyn's premature death spread like wildfire. So many out-of-towners reported that once they heard, they felt such a strong need to be here.

The wake commenced at a funeral parlor near their childhood home. The undertaker failed to recall a bigger turnout in recent memory. The receiving line snaked through the entire building and out the door (a two-hour wait for most of the night).

To Nick's credit, he greeted them all, never leaving his post, never sitting, never even taking a bathroom break. He stood the entire seven hours. Shared a tear with some, laughed with others. Meg and Mo stood with him for most of the evening, with Meg occasionally descending the long receiving line with her brothers and Caitlyn's dear friend Marie, to greet awaiting well-wishers.

The turnout of people who Caitlyn touched in some way overwhelmed everyone in attendance. You couldn't help but stand in awe and aspire to become a better person.

As the night swirled on, one lone man patiently stood in line with sad eyes and a heavy heart. He spoke to no one. Kept to himself. And as Meg walked the train, she immediately froze at the sight of this familiar, unmade bed.

The last time Meg saw him was standing in the doorway of their old St. Louis apartment, looking distraught and heartbroken, without the nest of gray hair he now sported.

Meg's heart swelled. Then she tenderly squeezed the hand of the man Caitlyn only referred to as KCO.

His distraught eyes glanced up, startled at first.

Meg smiled warmly. He returned the greeting.

"I'm so glad to see you," Meg said. "It would've meant

so much to her."

"I'm so sorry," his lips quivered. "I'm just...When I heard...It's so terrible. She was such a wonderful person."

"She'd be happy you came."

"I hear she had children."

"Two girls," Meg smiled.

A warm reminisce. "She always wanted children."

"Come here," Meg took his hand, and led him into one of the back rooms where the girls were playing with their McKenna cousins, not far from Irene's watchful eye. "There they are. That's Megan and Mary. Megan's 7 and Mary's 5."

"They look like her," he delighted. "They're beautiful."

"Megan, Mary," Meg called them over. "I want you to meet an old friend of your mom's."

"My mommy is with Jesus," Mary said.

"Yes she is, sweetie," KCO bent down to eye level. "It's nice to meet you both."

"Can we go home now?" Megan moaned.

Irene quickly stepped in. "They're getting tired. I was just about to take them back to the hotel."

"Mary Lou's going to take them back to her place in a little bit," Meg instructed. "Mo and I are staying there tonight."

"All their clothes are at the hotel," Irene resisted.

"Then go back to the hotel and grab their clothes," Meg stared her down.

"You don't want to have to worry about getting them dressed tomorrow morning with everything else going on," Irene said.

"That's exactly what we want to do," Meg smiled. "Now

why don't you take them to Mary Lou. Then you can go back to the hotel and get their things."

Irene pushed a smile and bit her tongue, escorting the girls to find Mary Lou.

When Meg turned to readdress KCO, she saw him by a table, staring at a candid picture of Caitlyn smiling and hamming it up.

"Did she have a happy life?" KCO asked.

"There was a lot of happiness in it," Meg offered, unable to answer more than that. "Her daughters made her happy."

His head bowed sadly. "She was the most beautiful person I ever knew."

Meg felt the unwavering love he carried for her sister all these years.

"I let fear get in the way. There were so many times I wanted to see her…" his voice trailed off regretfully. "What if, right…." he glanced at Meg with one of the saddest smiles she'd ever seen. "I'll always wonder 'what if.'" Then with choked words: "It would've been nice to hear her laugh one more time."

He was her Richard Joyce.

KCO smiled bravely before returning to his place in line.

Meg later spotted him kneeling before Caitlyn's casket. He rubbed his eyes, stood, turned, discretely wiped away tears, then quietly slipped through the crowd. That was the last time Meg saw the love of her sister's life.

As she watched him disappear into the throng of wake-goers, another sight caught her breath.

Robbie.

He was almost unrecognizable in a suit and tie, as he

fidgeted with it like a noose and straightjacket. He moved with a stiff gait, determined to walk without a cane. The scarring on his nose healed well. And the amputations to his fingertips were barely noticeable.

Before he saw her, Meg rushed to hug him (knocking him off balance in the process).

"Woo," he staggered on his prosthetics, regaining his footing.

"I'm sorry," Meg smiled, wanting to feel his arms around her. "You came."

"I'm so sorry about your sister," he said sincerely.

The hole Meg felt these last few months seemed to fill just being around him.

"Thanks for coming," Meg said. "It means a lot."

Robbie nodded. "She was a good person," Robbie said, eyes averted. "I'm sorry," he was no longer talking about Caitlyn. "I needed to know I could get better. I didn't want you to just be a caregiver the rest of your life…"

Meg shushed him and smiled. It was okay.

"Remember when I was out on Sister Island, in that coma? How I told you something made me open my eyes and get up."

"Yes."

"It was you. It was always you."

Meg stopped him with her finger over his lips. "I know."

They shared a warm smile and a laugh.

Then Robbie's expression turned sympathetic. "I heard about the shop. What are you going to do without it?"

"I don't know," Meg shrugged. "I haven't had time to think about it."

"Well, how about coming back to Door County so we can figure it out together?" Robbie asked hopefully.

Meg smiled warmly. "You'll be at the mass tomorrow?"

Robbie saw Meg wanted him there. "Sure."

"I'll see you then," Meg grinned, lingering on each other's smiles for a moment.

"See you then," Robbie grinned, and the two parted.

Meg turned back towards the receiving line and caught her mother's Irish eyes upon her. A warmth filled them both. Through all the past year's trials and tribulations, they appreciated enduring it together. It was just the two of them now. And their endearing smile conveyed the deep love they shared for one another.

Caitlyn's mass commenced the next morning at St. Peter's Church, where she and her siblings attended Catholic grade school. People packed it to the rafters. Meg and Nick stood on either side of the girls, with little Mary wearing a happy yellow dress to the funeral. "Yellow is mommy's favorite color, not black," she told Mo that morning. "Then wear yellow," Mo smiled. Irene was supposed to sit behind the family, but somehow ended up next to Nick fussing over the girls' every need. Nick and Meg offered eulogies. Meg fought to hold herself together. With tears in her eyes, she took the podium.

"Whenever things got too serious, Caitlyn always had an Irish joke," Meg started. "So…an Irishman, an Englishman and a Scotsman go into a pub. Each orders a pint of Guinness. Just as the bartender hands them over, three flies buzz down and land in each of the pints—one, two, three. The Englishman looks disgusted, pushes his pint away and demands another. The Scotsman picks out the fly, shrugs, and takes a long swallow. Then the Irishman reaches into the glass, grabs the fly between his fingers, and shakes him as hard as he can, shouting 'Spit it out, ya thievin' bastard! Spit it out!'"

The congregation laughed warmly, basking in the memory of their fallen comrade and Meg cast a soft smile to the heavens.

An hour later, they buried Caitlyn next to their beloved father. And it wasn't until that moment, when Meg watched her sister lowered into the ground that the full reality hit her: she'd never see Caitlyn again. They'd never share another laugh. Never lay under a blanket of stars with arms entwined. No more Chocolate Oirish Taters.

As the intimate gathering slowly trickled back to their cars, Meg remained at the grave. She stared blankly at the rectangular hole where her 35-year-old sister's body would forever rest. She wanted to pull Caitlyn out of the coffin and shake her back to life. She wasn't ready to give her up, until Mo tugged her gently, but firmly. It was time to let go.

Mary Lou held the reception at their St. Louis upper-middleclass Cape Cod-style home.

Meg and Mo allowed the rest of the McKenna clan to entertain guests while they played with Megan and Mary in the Fitzgibbons's large backyard.

They worried about Nick's custody of the girls and Irene assuming the role of mother. Neither could be trusted. But if they protested, Nick could make it difficult for them to see the girls—if not cut them off entirely. So, per their promise to Caitlyn, they bit their lip and played nice, keeping an acute eye and ear for any trouble, arranging as many visits as Nick would allow, and praying for the girls' safety. But both feared for the future and committed themselves to the girls' wellbeing.

"Your father is goin' to fly you both to Door County next month for Halloween," Mo said. "And we're all goin' to stay at Mary Lou's fer a whole week. How does that sound?"

"Will we gets to see the goats on the roof?" Mary lit up.

"Fer-sure-to-be-sure see the goats. And we'll eat ice cream…"

" — With the gumballs at the bottom!" Mary delighted.

"Is there another way? And we'll go trick-or-treatin', and make colcannon, and drink lamb's wool, and eat soul cakes, and carve turnips to scare away Stingy Jack…"

"What are turnips?"

"What are turnips? They're what people in Ireland carve instead of pumpkins. You know the Irish invented Halloween…" Mo went on to Mary's delight. "The Irish discovered America. Seven hundred years before Columbus they did…"

Across the backyard, Meg ambled over to Megan who sat alone at the far end of the property, sitting on a wrought-iron garden bench, staring blankly at the ground as she swung her legs back and forth. Meg sat down next to her. Both of them wore black dresses.

"It'll be okay, Megan."

Megan's eyes remained on her feet.

"Sometimes people just get sick, and there's nothing we can do about it. It's nobody's fault. Your mom didn't want to leave you girls. You know that. She loved you both very much."

Megan's eyes stared at the ground.

"You know you're flying out to see us next month for Halloween. Then we're flying up for New Year's. And we'll see you in February at your feis. Then you're going to fly to Door County right when you get out of school and spend three weeks with us at Mary Lou's."

Megan said nothing.

"Have you ever seen a leprechaun?"

"What?" Megan's eyes finally moved off her swinging feet and onto her Aunt Meg.

"A leprechaun," Meg smiled. "When I was little, I saw one in Door County."

"Nuh, uh," Megan looked skeptical.

"They say if you are born within five minutes of midnight you have the gift to see fairies and leprechauns when no one else can," Meg leaned closer to Megan and raised a twinkling brow. "You were born the same time as me."

The faintest hint of a smile appeared on Megan's face with this empowering revelation.

"Maybe both of us will get lucky and find a leprechaun when you visit," Meg gleamed. "I know just where to look for them."

Megan's eyes twinkled at the thought, and they both shared a warm smile.

CHAPTER 44

A CAITLYN ENDING

As dark as night gets, the day still comes.

—*Irish saying*

IN AN IRONIC TWIST OF FATE, Meg and Mo swapped roles in the months following Caitlyn's funeral. While Meg returned to Door County and planted roots with Robbie on Lighthouse Island, Mo turned into a pikey, hopping from city to city, a few months here, a few months there. Living with each of the children. Enjoying her grandchildren. Hanging out with Mary Lou. Spreading her Irishness wherever she landed. And like Meg, calling Megan and Mary no less than twice a week.

Meg sought solace in work: sketching, designing, stitching, and knitting (mostly clothes for her two nieces). Her big sister's candle that glowed so prominently in her life for over thirty years now left a cold void. Some days, when Meg sat alone in the quiet of the lighthouse tower, she felt Caitlyn's presence. Occasionally one of Caitlyn's silly Irish jokes echoed in her head. Sometimes her mind engaged in entire conversations with her big sister, usually about the girls, and they always ended with "I love you."

While Meg created her own fashion collection, Robbie rehabbed his legs exhaustively, determined to build up the strength and balance needed to defy his doctors and once again work his fishing rig.

At night, they made love by firelight. Played cards. Teased each other. They even improved Robbie's balance with Irish jigs that required him to hop on one foot.

Meg found an Irish shop in Chicago and one in St. Louis who bought most of Mo's remaining merchandise, while Mo's personal collection of Irish talismans and memorabilia remained boxed at Mary Lou's.

The girls visited for Halloween. Emmie Elefsson's Whitefish Creek Mercantile presented an elaborate Scandinavian scarecrow display of Vikings triumphantly sacking what Mo and Meg both surmised as Ireland.

The Historical Society cut a deal to move the Post Office into their old Irish shop at the top of Main Street, garnering the steady stream of rent needed to pay the loan they brokered to buy the place.

After Door County, Mo flew to Atlanta to spend two months with Meg's brother Tom, his wife, and their five kids.

Come Viking Season, Robbie reclaimed his title of Supreme Lutefisk to the thunderous applause of the crowd, setting a new Door County record of just over 7.2 pounds. And for Christmas, Meg made Megan and Mary exquisite, blue Irish dancing dresses, embroidered with their own unique weaves and stitching, that promised to turn all the

Irish dancing diehard coo-coo crazers green with envy.

Meg flew up to Boston for New Year's, where she, Mo, and Mary Lou enjoyed a fabulous week with the girls. They dined on Chocolate Oirish Taters. Then the trio ventured out on a memorable Little Christmas, carousing in Boston's Irish pubs until the wee hours, with Mo's legendary alter ego Lola throwing down pints of Guinness (or as Mo said "drownin' the shamrock"), swearing, playing tambourine, smacking arses, and stealing glassware from every pub.

They made it a point to order four pints at each bar they entered. One in Caitlyn's honor. And there it sat amidst all their joking, gossiping, and laughter until they each took turns sipping it dry as one of them retold one of Caitlyn's Irish jokes.

When Meg returned to the upper peninsula, Robbie announced his plans to fish again. He hired the Door Boys (two local brothers who Mary Lou swore were the most inept handymen in all Wisconsin) as second mates, and, as Robbie readily admitted, to help rescue him if he lost balance on his prosthetics and fell in.

A few weeks later, Meg cornered him with a scheming twinkle in her eye. "I've been thinking…"

"Uh, oh," Robbie grinned suspiciously. "What's that saying? When Irish eyes are smiling….Watch out."

"Well," Meg beamed with an impishly raised brow. "Now that you're fishing again, I have a business proposition…"

Robbie listened.

A week later, Meg turned Emmie Elefsson's world upside down. The former post office building's FOR SALE

OR LEASE sign came down, and on the white brick building's front doorway, tucked alongside Emmie's neighboring Whitefish Creek Mercantile, appeared the orange-white-and-green tri-striped flag of Ireland.

"How is yerself?" Meg asked as she paid a visit to her new neighbor.

Emmie Elefsson glared at Meg with a face that could turn milk sour.

Meg smiled. "I wanted to bring you some fresh-baked Irish raisin bread."

Emmie hissed. "You know where you can stick that."

"Alright then," Meg grinned. "Have a nice day."

Meg entered into a lease, negotiating for more favorable monthly payments and an allotment for all renovations. She contacted Mo's vendors and bargained for 90-day payment terms. One morning she showed up to find the Door Boys, Alewife Alma, Elsa Hedvig, Hat Guy, Nattie Bjorklunden and her husband Peder, and several other locals on her doorstep, voicing their disapproval of what the Historical Society did to them and offering to help rebuild her shop. "It's about time we had a little cultural diversity anyway," they grinned. And one of the first jobs they insisted to undertake was painting the front of the shop its orange-white-and-green tri-stripes.

Emmie Elefsson was fit to be tied.

Meg unboxed all Mo's Irish talismans and decorated the former post office just like their old shop, down to the *ring-a-ling-ling* of Mo's welcoming bell and the front doormat *Cead Mile Failte*. Meg designated a section for her own clothing line, then hung the old wooden sign, *All Things Irish*, and called Mo.

Two weeks later, Mo arrived. Without a word, she scrutinized the handwritten signs, the lucky horseshoes, Irish talismans, Meg's own clothing line of knits and dresses, and stopped cold at the large section of shameless Plastic Paddy trinkets, including shamrock-shaped dog dookie.

"No," Mo contested. "Absolutely not."

"These are big sellers."

"'Tis blatant Plastic Paddyism."

"You have to meet people where they are," Meg insisted. "And if this gets them in the door, so be it. Then you can teach them all about being Irish."

Mo thought about it for a moment. "Fine."

"So you'll be my partner?"

"No."

"No?" Meg startled. "But you're broke."

"O'im not broke."

"What do you mean? I saw your bank account — "

" — I still have me teacher's pension."

"But you lost the shop?"

A sly grin crept across Mo's face. "The shop was always fer you. I did it fer you."

Meg couldn't believe her ears.

"All the other kids we paid fer their college. You niver let us do that fer you. So I took all that money and started the shop. You were always so talented. This is what God called you to do."

Meg stood speechless.

"But if you'd be needin' some help, I think I could make meself available."

The two smiled at each other warmly. Then Meg hugged Mo. For the first time in a long while, they hugged together. Not out of fear or grief, but out of a shared love between mother and daughter.

On St. Patrick's Day, Megan and Mary flew in for a long weekend to join in the parade. Meg once again commandeered Robbie's flatbed trailer and convinced Chairman Philpot to issue a one-day liquor license to sell beer at the Irish shop, much to Emmie Elefsson's horror. Even Al Johnson loaned out a very special guest—Lars—to lead the parade (after he uncovered the identity of his goat's secret carrot supplier). And just as Meg taught Caitlyn the year before, she showed her two nieces how to pour a proper pint of Guinness. March 17th was a warm 49 degrees, and the girls jigged down Main Street in the beautiful dresses Meg made them. Paradegoers were sparse, but at least 40 people showed, and many more stood at the route's finish line outside the Irish shop where kegs of Guinness awaited. The shop enjoyed its best week of sales—selling the lot of *Kiss Me I'm Irish* shirts—and Meg knew Caitlyn was smiling.

Ring-a-ling-ling.

Booker walked in.

"Ladies," he meandered around the shop.

Booker picked out a shillelagh, taking a few test swings, and saw Mo eyeing him like a sniper.

"Relax, I'm not going to steal it."

"You'd steal the sugar from a cup of tea," Mo glared.

Booker held up the shillelagh. "This is a good one."

He strolled to the counter.

"You still owe me for the last one you stole," Mo said.

"And I plan to pay for it today," he grinned, handing them cash. "Do you have this month's rent?"

"Here you go," Meg handed him the envelope.

"What is he talkin' about?" Mo asked.

Booker grinned. "Looks like I'm your new landlord."

"Jaysus, Mary and Joseph," Mo exclaimed, turning fiercely on Meg. "You made a deal wid the divil!"

Booker's smile stretched into a wolfish grin. "You interested in making a deal with the devil, too?"

"Yer disgustin'. Get out of me shop."

Booker cackled. "See you around," and he waved one of his gloved hands as he walked out.

"Well at least he paid for his shillelagh," Mo proudly informed Meg.

"Did he pay for the drinking gloves he was wearing on his hands?" Meg asked.

"Bollix!" Mo cursed him.

After the girls flew back to Boston with a whole suitcase full of Irish gifts, Meg and Robbie sailed out on his boat to watch the setting sun paint a magnificent, cloudy sky.

"I have something for you," Robbie handed Meg an opened envelope.

"What is it?" Meg asked.

"Look," Robbie motioned inside.

Meg looked at the address. It was Robbie's. But the return address was somewhere in Ireland.

"What is this?" she pulled out the letter inside.

"Just read it."

Meg glanced up at him in surprise and disbelief, then opened the letter, which had another attached.

Dear Mr. Knudson—

Normally we are prohibited from giving the information you requested. But I knew the name of the person you inquired about. I was able to locate the file. And did find one letter. I think this will answer a lot of your questions. Please give Meg my best. ☺

God bless,
Mother Superior

Meg smiled at the memory of Mother Superior. Then took the attached letter.

Dear Mother Superior—

I can never repay you for what you have given us. The last ten years of miscarriages and trying to have a child have been the hardest of my life. I had started to lose faith. I know you probably frown on making contact with the mother, but if she ever asks, please let her know how grateful and forever in her debt I am. I cannot imagine the emotional difficulty of giving up a child. Nor the courage or sacrifice it takes. It is an incredible leap of faith. I can only thank her from the bottom of my heart. She has given us a family. Something I will never be able to repay. Let her know how much her child is loved by us all, her cousins, aunts, uncles and grandparents. She is so very happy. She loves to laugh and has a mystical way about her. Sometimes I think she can see angels. I thank God every day for our Keira and for her mother's sacrifice. God bless. You answered our prayer. Thank you for blessing us with this wonderful child.

With teary eyes, joy swelled inside Meg like a balloon. Even Robbie turned misty eyed.

"A girl," she smiled. "We had a girl."

Meg felt at peace.

They hugged for a long time, then stared out at the sunset.

"There's one more thing," Robbie grinned, reached into his pocket, and pulled out a ring.

But not just any ring—a Claddagh.

And not just any Claddagh, but her family's—Caitlyn's.

Meg did a double take. "How did you get that?"

"Your sister mailed it to me," Robbie smiled, holding the Claddagh and grabbing her left hand. "She mailed it shortly before she passed away. Said it's Irish tradition for the girl to be given this by the guy."

Robbie took Meg's hand and stumbled on his prosthetics as he stepped closer to slip it on her finger.

The ring fumbled out his hand.

Meg watched horrified as several centuries of her family's most sacred heirloom flipped over the railing and, almost in slow motion, plunked into the lake.

"Oh my God!" Meg gasped, diving after it without a second thought.

"Oh God!" She frantically splashed in 40-foot deep water, diving, filling her lungs.

Robbie started laughing.

"You're laughing?" Meg was sick about it. "How can you be laughing?"

"That was a fake," he laughed harder. "I had the jeweler make it for me. I just wanted to see your face."

"That was just cruel!" Meg swam quickly to the boat's ladder ready to toss him in the second she climbed aboard, when Robbie produced another gold ring.

"Here's the real one," he smiled.

The sight of Caitlyn's ring wiped away any ferocity. It was indeed their family's coveted Claddagh. And before Meg could say another word, Robbie slipped it onto her left ring finger.

"That's wrong," Meg attempted to pull away.

"What?" Robbie glanced up confused.

"The heart's facing inwards," Meg pointed to the heart on the Claddagh. "On the left hand, that means you're married. The right hand means you're in a relationship. Outwards on the left hand means you're engaged."

Meg started to pull it off.

Robbie stopped her. "I think it looks good the way it is," he smiled.

Meg grinned at the Claddagh, thinking of her sister looking out for her.

She turned to Robbie and they met in a deep, loving kiss that could've lasted days, if not for a gull that shat on their heads.

They pulled back to see the laughter in each other's face.

Irish luck.

Find the Author:

website:	http://michaelloynd.com/
blog:	http://michaelloynd.com/blog/
facebook:	Michael Loynd
	All Things Irish
twitter:	miloynd
	allthingsirish

24937316R00147

Made in the USA
Lexington, KY
08 August 2013